RESTLESS

Other books by Stan Rogal

short stories
What Passes for Love

poetry
The Ermerald City
The Imaginary Musuem
Sweet Betsy from Pike
Personations

RESTLESS

Stan Rogal

INSOMNIAC PRESS

Copyright © 1998 by Stan Rogal.

All rights reserved. No part of this publication may be reproduced, stored in a retrieval system or transmitted, in any form or by any means, without the prior written permission of the publisher or, in case of photocopying or other reprographic copying, a licence from CANCOPY (Canadian Copyright Licensing Agency), 6 Adelaide St. E., Suite 900, Toronto, Ontario, Canada, M5C 1H6.

Edited by Mike O'Connor
Copy edited by Lloyd Davis & Liz Thorpe
Designed by Mike O'Connor

Canadian Cataloguing in Publication Data

Rogal, Stan, 1950-
  Restless

ISBN 1-895837-19-7

I. Title.

PS8585.O391R47 1998   C813'.54   C98-930289-X
PR9199.3.R63R47 1998

Printed and bound in Canada

Some of these stories have appeared previously in *Zygote*, *Smoke*, *The Carleton Arts Review*, *Carousel*, *Quarry Press Anthology: Best Canadian Murder/Mystery Stories* and *Missing Jacket*.

The publisher gratefully acknowledges the support of the Ontario Arts Council.

Insomniac Press
393 Shaw Street, Toronto, Ontario, Canada, M6J 2X4
www.insomniacpress.com

What the Women Don't Know
11

Is That You?
25

A Trick of Light
35

The Regular
49

Restless and Fleeting
55

Passenger
67

Dress Rehearsal
73

Scene at a Bus Stop
83

Three Sketches Toward a Self-Portrait by Sigmund Freud:

White   *89*
Red   *101*
Black   *115*

Beached
125

Selene
131

Notes
151

This book is dedicated to all those friends whose lives I've fragmented, then rearranged and altered in order to create what is commonly called fiction.

Special thanks to Mike O'Connor for his continued belief and support as well as to Jacquie Jacobs for providing both art and inspiration.

List of artwork

1 *Missing All Over*, oil, 122 cm x 90 cm, p. 11

2 *Once Removed*, ink and charcoal, 90 cm x 58 cm, p. 25

3 *Tossed & Turned*, oil, 127 cm x 95 cm, p. 35

4 *Storm Front* (study), collage, 11 cm x 20 cm, p. 49

5 *Absence*, charcoal and acrylic paint, 47 cm x 28 cm, p. 55

6 *Homo Carbo*, ink and charcoal, 90 cm x 55 cm, p. 67

7 *Freefall*, oil, 70 cm x 70 cm, p73

8 *Between Beats*, charcoal and acrylic paint, 40 cm x 57 cm, p.85

9 *Narcissus (triptych)*, oil, 125 cm x 180 cm, p. 89

10 *Narcissus (triptych) #1*, oil, 125 cm x 60 cm, p. 91

11 *Narcissus (triptych) #2*, oil, 125 cm x 60 cm, p. 103

12 *Narcissus (triptych) #3*, oil, 125 cm x 60 cm, p. 117

13 *Leda*, charcoal and acrylic paint, 40 cm x 57 cm, p. 127

14 *Treading*, oil, (trapezoid), 100 cm top, 77 cm bottom, 110 cm height, p. 133

I had hoped, by means of the bouquet of flowers, to appease my love
for her a little. It was quite useless. It is possible only through
literature or through sleeping together. I write this not because I did
not know it, but rather because it is perhaps well to write
down warnings frequently.
— *Franz Kafka*

You've never had a face
but you know that appeals to me.
— *Margaret Atwood*

All the black same I dance
my blue head off...
— *John Berryman*

WHAT THE WOMEN DON'T KNOW
— for Lou Reed

The two men had been drinking for a couple of hours. It'd started quietly enough with a bottle of wine over dinner with Julie, Mike's wife, Gerry's sister, but once on their own, they'd settled in to drink in earnest.

"What sort of shithole dive did you drag me into, anyway?" Gerry mumbled the words like some two-bit movie mafioso type. He checked out the room. He'd been checking out the room since they arrived, half expecting it to change. It hadn't.

"What do you mean?" Mike drew a last drag from his cigarette and squashed the butt into an already full ashtray.

"I mean, look around you — the place is fucking dead. I figured you'd take me somewhere where there'd be some action."

"What sort of action?" Mike lit another smoke.

"Female action. A groovy bar. A club. A strip joint maybe. I don't know. Place is like a biker bar. You gotta empty your own fucking ashtray, for fuck's sake." Gerry dumped the contents beside two other piles of ashes and crushed filters on the next table. "You know what I'm saying?"

"You're a married man, remember? To my sister, no less. Besides, there's always a free table here and the beer's cheap."

"And you're married to my sister — so what? What the women don't know won't hurt us, right?" Mike laughed at his own joke. "Anyway, I'm not out to get laid, just have a little fun, y'know? A few drinks, a little conversation..."

"Isn't that what we're having?" Mike leaned back and blew a half-dozen smoke rings. He wasn't much of a talker, actually. He knew that. His forté was playing straight man or devil's advocate. Gerry was the one with the gift of the gab.

"It's my last night in the big city, pal. I want to have a good time. Back home in the Sault you can't even sneeze without twenty nice, polite folks shouting bless you and handing you a fucking kleenex. Here, you walk three or four blocks in any direction and you're anonymous. No one knows you, no one cares. You can do what you want."

Gerry worked for Bell as a troubleshooter and was down from Sault Ste Marie for a training course. Part of his job entailed upgrading on a regular basis. The training locations varied, but more often than not, it was Toronto.

"I thought you guys liked living in the sticks."

"I don't mind it. Karen loves it. She was only too happy to get me away from what she calls 'the bad element'."

"Meaning?"

"Meaning good pals like you who were always leading me away from the straight and narrow."

"As if you ever needed help on that score."

Gerry laughed and pointed at Mike. "Exactly. But it was great having someone else to lay the blame on."

"So now you've got no excuse."

"I also got no opportunity, so it doesn't really matter." Gerry swung around in his chair. "What about them? What do you think?" He tipped his glass in the direction of two women chalking up cues at the pool table.

Mike took a quick glance then squinted his eyes clear for a double take. "You crazy? Either you need your eyes examined or your head. They gotta be dykes."

"So?" Gerry clicked his tongue.

"So? So what's the point? You just wanna piss them off, or what?"

"Maybe it's the old story — they haven't met the right guy." Gerry laughed and banged back his beer. "C'mon. Let's do it. We'll go over and shoot some pool with them; yak it up a bit. Might be interesting. What do you say?"

"What's the matter? They got no dykes in the Sault?"

"Not in fucking Denny's, which is about the height of a social evening up there." Gerry divided the remainder of the pitcher into the two glasses. "What say we order a couple of shots, eh? Tequila. This beer's starting to bloat me." He burped.

"Not for me. I can't handle the hard stuff any more."

"You know your problem? You're getting old. And fat. You must've put on ten pounds since I saw you last." Gerry shot a fist across the table and poked Mike in the stomach. "And you were packin' extra then. It's this shitty beer you drink. I bet you come in here every other night for a few and just sit on your ass. You're thirty-two going on a hundred — like those dumb fuckers I work with. All they can talk about is what they're gonna do with all the time they'll have when they retire at fifty-five. You know what they'll do? Nothin', just like now. You know what I say? Use it or lose it."

"Sounds like a good thing Karen keeps you on a short leash."

"Yeah. No telling what might happen. I might enjoy myself for a change."

Mike waved for another pitcher. "You having problems at home? With Karen? Is that what you're telling me?" The waiter dropped the beer at the table. Gerry fished around in his pocket but Mike had a twenty ready and tossed it onto the tray. "My shout," he said.

"No. No problems. Things are pretty good actually. I'm just sounding off. Maybe it's being in Toronto, maybe it's the beer, maybe…" Gerry downed his glass and poured another. "I don't know. Fuck it."

Mike toyed with the ashtray. "You sure there's nothing you want to tell me? I mean, Karen's my sister, but you and me go back a long way." He hesitated. "Shit, I remember we used to go down to the woods and beat each other off." He laughed a low laugh that could either be taken as dismissive or nostalgic. Hard to tell.

Gerry stared straight at Mike. "Don't even remind me, OK?" He didn't sound angry. He did sound serious. "That was a long time ago." There was a brief silence. Mike picked up his beer. Gerry burped lightly then massaged his brow with his hand. "We were just kids, for chrissakes." He spoke into the red fabric that covered the table.

Mike tapped the ash from his cigarette. "Yeah. Kids."

Gerry gave his head a shake, let out a sound like a growl, then laughed. "Anyhow… the point is… we're trying to make-a-the-baby and it ain't happening. We've been trying for about a year. Not even close."

"Ah. You go in and get checked out?"

"Karen went in. Came back certified A-1 baby-making material."

"You?"

Gerry shrugged. "I've been... putting it off. I don't know, I just can't get my head around jerking off into a plastic bottle and then have some doctor tell me there ain't enough lead in my pencil to sign my name, y'know?"

"Doesn't have to be the end of the world. Me and Julie don't have kids."

"Yeah, but you're down here in the city. Up there things are different. Everybody has kids. Their whole social life revolves around kids. If you don't have kids they look at you as if something's wrong. They get suspicious. It's like you're not a real man unless you produce some kind of living proof."

"You're exaggerating."

"Don't bet on it. They're friendly enough up front, but behind our backs they call us 'that poor young couple.'" Gerry anticipated Mike's next question and stopped him with a raised finger. "I've overheard them talking. It's like they're afraid."

"Afraid of what?"

"I don't know. Maybe that they'll get infected. Maybe that their world isn't as safe as they thought. My good buddies look at me like maybe I can't get it up; like maybe..." Gerry sipped his beer. Mike looked on, not sure whether to press the issue, change the subject or keep his mouth shut. He wasn't used to seeing Gerry in this way — searching for words; struggling with thoughts. Gerry lifted his head and gave Mike a wide grin. "And it's probably all your fault, you fucker."

"My fault?"

"Yeah. That stuff in the woods. That was your idea." Mike gave his neck a stretch and licked his lips. "You even tried to get me to suck your cock once. I remember that."

"Like you said, we were just kids."

"Maybe, but I'll tell you — for a time back then, I don't know... thirteen, fourteen, fifteen years old — whatever, I wasn't sure if I was a Gerald or a Geraldine."

"Everyone goes through some kind of identity crisis at that age. It's not unusual." Mike lit a cigarette. "You got through it OK, right? You're a married man."

Gerry nodded. "That's right. I did. Like I say, I'm just sounding off." Someone dropped a coin into the jukebox and Gerry began pounding the table to the rhythm. "Those things are gonna kill you, you know that?"

Mike inhaled. "Yeah," he said. "Most likely."

"I'm kidding. Smoke your brains out. You only go around once, might as well do what you want while you have the chance. Shit, things are getting way too fucking serious here. I'm gonna order us a couple of tequilas. We're gonna get stinko. It's my last night." Gerry turned to find the waiter. "Hey," he stopped. "What do you make of that?" A woman entered from upstairs. Gerry guessed her to be at least fifty or sixty, maybe older. She was a big woman. Heavy, though not fat; solid, full-figured and firmly rounded. She had a head of platinum-blonde hair and her face was a mask of thick make-up. She wore a tight-fitting, low-cut lamé gown and her body was adorned with beads, glitter and gaudy jewellery.

"That's Connie Lake," said Mike. "She owns the place."

"Does she always come in dressed like that?"

"She's not in that often. Only when the mood strikes her."

"She looks like she stepped out of a '50s flick."

"She was an actress back then. Nothing big. Bit parts. She played a waitress across from Robert Mitchum in *Clouds of Glory*. Apparently she made the rounds with a lot of leading men in her day. Never really made it in the business, though."

"Why not?"

"Personal problems. Booze, drugs, getting caught once too often with the wrong man in the wrong place. The usual."

"How do you know so much about her?"

Gerry picked up his glass and drank. "I asked the same questions you did when I first saw her."

"She still looks pretty good, in a perverse sort of way. I'll bet there's a lot of life in the old girl yet. What do you think — when's the last time she got laid?"

"You wanna fuck her?"

"Fuck, no. She's old enough to be my mother. I'm curious. I just wanna, you know, have a little fun with her. Give her a good time." Gerry twisted in his chair. "I'm gonna go over and buy her a drink."

"She might be more than you can handle."

"Are you kidding me? *Clouds of Glory*, right? I remember seeing it on the late night show awhile back. Robert Mitchum was some down-on-his-luck, alcoholic, ex-fighter pilot." The woman stuck a cigarette into a holder. "Christ," Gerry whistled softly. "I don't believe it." He grabbed a pack of matches from the table. "What do you think she drinks?"

"Try bourbon."

"Bourbon? Right." Gerry crossed the room, lighting a match and ordering drinks along the way.

Mike took a last, long, hard drag and lit a second cigarette with the one that was already going. Pig fucking, he thought. That's what they called it when he was a teenager — lighting one cigarette with another. Pig fucking. Where'd we come up with that one? he wondered. We were just kids. He poured himself more beer and sat back to catch the show.

He had always enjoyed seeing Gerry at work. The guy was a sweet talker, no doubt about it. Mike was familiar with his style from years back, those days before marriage when they'd hit the bars and parties together. He could imagine the conversation taking place. Gerry introducing himself, offering the drink, her asking how he knew she drank bourbon, him saying it was like he knew from looking at her — the way she moved, her style — and what was her name and was she the same Connie Lake who was the actress and didn't she play opposite Robert Mitchum in *Clouds of Glory*? Great film, et cetera, and he remembers her as the waitress and thought she was terrific, et cetera, and there's no such thing as small roles only small actors and she had definite screen presence, et cetera, et cetera... There was a second round of drinks and the body language progressed quickly to mouths leaning closer to ears and casual brushes of hands to elbows and bodies drawing generally nearer — to overcome the interference, you understand: pool balls breaking, dishwasher running, jukebox playing, customer voices swelling in direct proportion to the amount of alcohol consumed. Et cetera. Mike wasn't too surprised when

Gerry headed over to fill him in on the latest development.

"Connie's invited me up to look at her photo collection. Movie stills and shit. She lives upstairs of this dump, can you believe it? I'm gonna go have a look-see. Shouldn't be long." He raised his eyebrows and grinned. "How long can it take to see a coupla dusty old photos, eh? Hang tough and don't leave without me, OK?" He dropped a twenty on the table. "Order us another pitcher."

Mike made a revolver with his hand and pointed the barrel at Mike. He clicked his tongue. "You got it." Gerry crossed the floor, wrapped an arm around Connie's waist and escorted her up the stairs. The last thing Mike saw were Gerry's sneakers. The were doing a sort of drunken soft-shoe.

The apartment was every bit as outrageous as Connie herself. The place was decked out in gold brocade and trim with brightly coloured furniture and oversized sofas. Between the gilt-framed mirrors, the photos and movie posters, Gerry saw that the walls had been ragged in pinks, purples and burgundies. Not to his taste, thought Gerry, but definitely a fashion statement. He stood in front of a picture. It was a shot of Lee Marvin with his arm locked around a pretty, young blonde. Was it Connie? Gerry wondered. It wasn't impossible. He leaned in to read the inscription: *To my sweet Connie, love Lee.* "Son of a bitch," Gerry whistled under his breath. He studied the faces of other past leading men hung around the room.

"Were you... friends with all these guys.?"

"Friends?"

"I mean, were you, I guess, intimate?"

"You mean, did I fuck them all?" Connie waved her cigarette toward a bottle and glasses on the bar. "There's bourbon in the decanter. Why don't you pour us a drink?" She picked up a silver cigarette case from the coffee table and opened it. "I'll light us up a joint. You do inhale, don't you?" One side of her mouth curled a slight smile. Gerry nodded. "There's coke if you prefer. In the box." She indicated an ornately carved teak box also on the coffee table.

"Grass is fine." Gerry handed her a drink. They clinked glasses, chin-chin, then sat on the couch and passed the joint.

"No. I didn't fuck them all." She allowed her eyes to slowly scan the walls. "Most of them." The words were spoken simply, sort of matter-of-factly.

"What about the Duke?" Gerry took a deep hit.

"John was into blow-jobs. He felt that as long as he didn't stick it in, it wasn't really sex, therefore he wasn't really cheating." She inhaled.

Gerry's eyes widened as he coughed the smoke from his lungs. "You gave John Wayne a blow-job?" He laughed, took another hit and held it.

"Several." Connie pursed her lips.

"Wow," said Gerry, passing the joint. "This grass has gone straight to my head."

"It's elephant grass. It takes some getting used to."

"Yeah, I'd say it packs a punch." Gerry gave his head a shake. He threw back the bourbon and tipped the glass on the table. "I think I'm ripped," he grinned.

"Mm." Connie set her drink beside Gerry's glass. "So — Gerry — why are you here, exactly?" She asked the question flat-out, catching Gerry off-guard.

"Uh... I told you. I'm down on a course." His tongue traced out his lips. He was having trouble focusing.

"I mean here. In my bar, in my room. With me now. Why exactly are you here? What are you after?" Again, her words were spoken directly, without emotion, almost businesslike.

"Nothing. Honest. What do you think?"

"Oh, I don't know Gerry. A good-looking young man out on his own in the big city — maybe you bought a ticket to *Sunset Boulevard* and thought it might be a hoot to go out and take advantage of an aging, washed-out former movie actress."

"No. I wouldn't do that." The grass really had gone to his head. He was thinking that maybe he should get up and leave. On the other hand, there was something about Connie that made him want to stay. The way she presented herself, perhaps. Perhaps her confidence.

"That's good to hear, Gerry. 'Cause we both know what happened to that other young man, don't we?"

"He got shot."

"Precisely. And it was the old actress that shot him, isn't that right?"

"Yeah, well…" He let out a small, uncomfortable laugh.

"Or maybe you were once a Boy Scout and you decided to perform a good deed by giving an old woman a final go before she kicks off." Connie placed the extinguished joint in the ashtray. She brushed an invisible strand of hair from her cheek. "Or maybe the idea was to tease me, then bugger off when I begged for more, which wouldn't be very nice either, would it?"

"No. No, it wouldn't. And I didn't. I was just out for some fun. I thought you'd be fun to be with."

"And aren't I fun?"

"Yeah. I mean, you were, but…"

"But you don't find me attractive."

"I never said that. I do find you attractive. Very."

"You do? How sweet." She inhaled and slid closer to him, pressing her chest against his. "You don't find my old body too repulsive?"

"You've got a terrific body. There's women that'd kill for a body like yours. Younger women, even." He rested the back of his hand gently between her breasts.

"They used to be the best that money could buy."

"Nothing wrong with them now." He turned his hand and teased the spot where a nipple showed through the dress. The two embraced and kissed. Gerry continued caressing Connie's breasts as she drove her tongue into his open mouth. After a time, Gerry pulled back for air. "Whoa. You sure know how to kiss."

"Practice makes perfect," she said. They went back at it. Gerry's hand slipped down past Connie's waist and headed between her legs. She stopped him. "Not so fast. I'm just getting warmed up."

She undid Gerry's shirt and sucked on his nipples. She unzipped his pants and placed her mouth over his erection. Gerry thought that she was also very good at this, not soft and slow like other women he had known, but hard and fast. Connie was in complete control; there was nothing for Gerry to do but sit back and enjoy the ride. A smile crossed his face. He saw John Wayne staring at him. Bastard, thought Gerry. Dirty old bastard. Then he came.

Connie swished a heavy shot of bourbon around in her mouth and swallowed. "Mm," she sighed, throwing back her head and grinning. "Was it good for you, too?"

Gerry cupped her face, kissed her and leaned her into the couch. He moved a hand to her knee and began working it up her thigh. "It was great. You're incredible. Now I want to do something nice for you." His hand disappeared beneath the hem of her dress.

"Are you sure, Gerry?" She gripped her glass behind Gerry's neck as he nuzzled her breasts. "I mean to say — a woman of my age — you never know what you might find."

Gerry's hand travelled from Connie's thigh, to her hip, to her belly and downward. Reaching her crotch, he suddenly froze. "Oh Christ," he whispered. There was a tremor in his voice. He bolted off of the couch. As he stood his head spun and he staggered toward the door. He fumbled with his shirt buttons; with the zipper in his pants. "Oh, Christ." Tears formed in the corners of his eyes.

Connie sat up and adjusted the hem of her dress. She sipped her bourbon. "Don't behave like such a child, Gerry. As you can see," she made a flourish with her arm, "you're among excellent company. You should feel flattered. Now you have a story to tell the boys at home. You shared an experience with the Duke." She smiled, then immediately dropped it. "But maybe you were wanting a different sort of experience. Is that it?" She removed the blonde wig, straightened a few strands of hair, then carefully replaced it on her head. The coyness left her voice. "Good night, Gerry. Come back any time."

Gerry had his back against the door. He didn't know what to do; didn't know what to say. He didn't know whether to simply walk out or scream or pick up the decanter and go over and bash in Connie's skull. He glanced again at the pictures on the wall. Had Connie, had she — had he — ever been with these men? Ever been in the movies? Ever been to Hollywood, even? And there was something else, another question having to do with... what? He tried to think back, but his brain refused to cooperate, whether because of the booze or the drugs or... Something that he couldn't put his finger on. Then there was Connie, calm as a garish Buddha, freshening her make-up and smoking a cigarette. Had any of this really happened? How could she look at him that way, with such seeming unconcern?

"I'm not a fag," he said, finally. "I'm a happily married man."
"I'm sure," said Connie.
"I won't be back."
"Of course you won't." Gerry opened the door to leave. "And Gerry," Connie called. "Say hello to Mike for me, will you? And tell him…" She dipped her pinkie into the bourbon and slipped the wet tip into her mouth. She sucked it for a moment with her lips, then withdrew it. "Tell him not to be such a stranger."

Gerry stumbled into the hall. He pulled the door toward him, but didn't shut it all the way. Connie's eyes were fixed on him. She took a lipstick from her purse. Gerry dropped to his knees and pressed his face to the crack in the door. He watched as Connie applied the colour to her lips; watched her lips pucker and pout. He thought about where the lips had been. He thought, also, about Mike, waiting for him downstairs. He couldn't move from the spot; couldn't help himself. He knew that. There was nothing he could do.

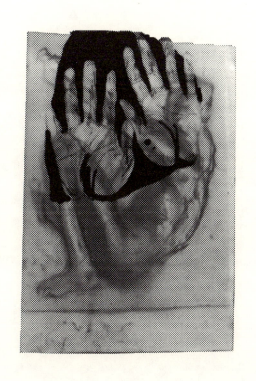

IS THAT YOU?

Paul was the last person Frank had expected to find sitting there. Or, if not the last, at least a close second. Maybe he shouldn't have thought that way. After all, who was he to judge what people did with their time? Still, circumstances being what they were, and Paul seeming to be so into making things work, it was a surprise.

"This seat taken?" Frank lowered himself onto the bar stool next to Paul. It was late, after eleven, Washington was playing Atlanta on the TV — a mean-nothing game — and the place was practically deserted. "How ya doin'? What's up? Long time no see."

It took a few seconds for Paul to register the presence of the second man, and when he did, he didn't appear to recognize him immediately. "Frank," he said.

"You watching the game?"

"Hm?"

"The game." Frank nodded his chin toward the screen.

"Oh, yeah."

"What's the score?"

"The score?" Paul gave it some thought, then shook his head. "I don't know. I guess I lost track. I mean, I wasn't really paying attention, y'know? I'm just…"

"It's just there. I know. I'm the same way. Turn the bastard on and you can't help but look at it." Frank laughed. There was no reaction from Paul. "You OK?"

"Sure. Fine. Never better. Why?" Paul finished his drink and lit a cigarette. The waiter came over, emptied the ashtray. Paul motioned for another rum and Coke and Frank ordered a beer.

"I was just wondering. I mean, to tell the truth," Frank did a quick calculation in his head, "I didn't expect to see you here. So soon, I mean. I more or less assumed... you know..."

"Yeah, well." Paul tapped the side of his glass with his fingers. As it stood, the conversation was going nowhere and Frank knew it. He tried a different approach.

"Can I bum a smoke?"

"I thought you quit?"

"I thought we both quit." Frank felt some faint glimmer of hope in Paul's response, but this quickly vanished. The man simply shrugged and pushed the pack in Frank's direction. Frank lit up, inhaled and gave a slight cough. There was no point in pressing the issue, he thought. If Paul wanted to talk, he'd talk. If he didn't, that was up to him. He'd been given ample opportunity and Frank felt that the two weren't close enough friends to just come out and ask. They had met through a previous job. Now they bumped into each other once in awhile. Usually here, over drinks. They were acquaintances, that was it. No, best to wait and see. Smoke a cigarette, have a beer, and if nothing happened, go home. What the hell — they hadn't even seen each other for about, what, seven months? On the other hand, if there'd been problems — complications? The story was familiar enough. You hear about it every day. Couples who, for whatever reason, are unable to have kids. The biological clock is ticking. You try everything; spend years, maybe, and lots of cash. All the latest medical advances, New Age theories, even witchcraft, if you're desperate enough — who knows? Nothing works. Finally you give up, it's hopeless, and, bingo, like that you're pregnant. The perfect example: Paul just over forty and his wife closing in.

Frank saw the change. Paul was tickled. He quit smoking. In fact, the two had made a pact the same night. Paul also had his last drink — until after the baby, he said. He quit going out after work altogether. It was all what's best for the wife and baby now. Proper diet, exercise, prenatal classes — the whole nine yards.

That was the last time the two men had seen each other, when Paul laid out his plans for a new life. The way Frank figured, the baby should have arrived by now. Paul should be home right now hugging his wife and making funny faces to his newborn. Instead, here he was sitting in a bar near midnight, getting ripped on rum and Cokes. Not that Frank couldn't relate to needing a little space now and again. He'd been through two wives and had kids with both of them. There was nothing easy about raising a family, for sure. But that was later, after the thrill was gone, so to speak, and reality had set in. So, maybe it was the other thing. You do your best, whatever's humanly possible, and it turns out it wasn't meant to be after all. Not unusual. Not these days. Shit happens, thought Frank. Only, it's not supposed to happen to you. He put out his cigarette and thought about ordering another beer.

"What do you think it is that happens, eh?" It was Paul speaking, but the voice had turned somehow foreign, as if dragged from some deep space. Not 'deep', philosophically, but as if from a source buried away far inside the body; cold, flat, articulate.

"I don't know. What do you mean?" asked Frank. Paul wasn't listening, that was plain. Somewhere inside his head, a reel of film had kicked in and he was about to let it play. Maybe for the first time; maybe for the hundredth. Frank drew a second cigarette from the pack and lit it.

"You do everything you're supposed to do. You listen to all of the advice. You don't take any chances. You bust your ass to make sure things are right. And so it goes. Everything smooth. On schedule. No problems. A piece of cake. Right up to the time." Paul moves his glass in a circle on the counter. He sighs. "They make it so you know exactly what to expect. No surprises. You see it on the screen a dozen times and it's no worse than watching the evening news. Or a movie. So... what happens? What the fuck happens?" He drained his glass then gave the ice a rattle as a signal to the bartender.

"I was there, eh. Right in the delivery room with her. Holding her hand. Telling her to breathe; telling her to relax; telling her everything's going to be OK. What else can the man do? Nothing. I felt useless as shit. Meanwhile, she's lying there on a table with her legs spread and she's hurtin'. She's in pain, right? She's pushin' and she's pushin', but nothin's happening. She's been going at it for hours now, she's exhausted, but she keeps pushing. And she's screaming. She's screaming like she's going to die. She wants to die. She wants it over. She never wants to go through this again. It's all my fault, she says. She'll never fuck again; she'll never let a man touch her again. I've never heard her like this. I've never seen her like this. It's like she's another person. Someone I've never met. I don't recognize her."

Paul reached for a cigarette, then stopped. "About the time I thought things couldn't get any worse, the baby's head starts popping out. Everyone's back at it, telling her to push. She lets out this wail that doesn't sound human. Honest to God, it's like she's possessed or something. The air turns blue. She's swearing at everyone, everything — fuck this, fuck that, fucking Christ — the works. She's screaming at the doctor to cut her open, she can't take any more. At this point, I'm losing it. I'm sick. My head's spinning. I'm sweating like a pig. I can't talk." He raised a cigarette to his lips and Frank lit it.

"One of the doctors is crouched down between her legs. He's rubbing her with a finger; massaging her around the baby's head. The head's just stuck there. In his other hand, he's holding a scalpel. He's saying to Karen, 'Look, you don't want a Caesarean and neither do I. You're doing great. Just push. One more time. Push.'" Paul took another drag and a drink. His tone shifted.

"Don't let anyone ever tell you these guys don't care. They were there for Karen the whole time. Cool as cucumbers, right? Professional. But there for her. Caring. Wanting to help her through it all. One of the nurses was finished her shift but she said she wasn't leaving until she knew that the baby was born and everything was all right. It's something you don't hear about often enough." He pulled at his jaw. "I'll tell you something else — women aren't the weaker sex. They have more guts, more strength..." His voice broke. "Honest to God, you just never know, until..." Paul hesitated.

"Anyway, the baby's not coming and the baby's not coming. Apparently there's not enough dilation and he's caught up behind the pelvic bone. Again, the doctor says one more time, 'Push.' And just as Karen gives it her all, he takes the scalpel and slits her. Nothing big, a quick slit to open her wider, but there's blood everywhere. It's as if he'd cut her from asshole to breakfast, y'know? The blood is gushing. Where does it come from? I have no idea." Paul went silent, as though he was talked out. As though he had nothing more to say on the subject.

"What happened then?" Frank asked.

"Then? I passed out. When I came to, it was all over."

"What about the baby? And Karen?"

"Fine. Both fine. It was a boy." Paul finished his rum and Coke and called for the bill.

"That's great."

"Yeah. Yeah — great."

Frank was still puzzled and he wondered whether or not he should ask anything more. Normally, he would've let it go. He didn't like to stick his nose where it didn't belong, especially when it came to family matters. But, if anyone needed a friend right now, or simply a shoulder, it seemed to be Paul.

"You can tell me if it's none of my business, but what are you doing here when you've got a wife and a young son at home waiting for you?"

Paul leaned his head back and clenched his teeth. A few tears squeezed from his eyes and he wiped them away with the back of his hand. Frank sat like a statue, wondering what the hell was going on.

"I can't. I can't face her. Not after…"

"After what? You passed out, so what? That's nothing to be ashamed of. Lots of men don't make it through the delivery. Lots don't even try. At least you tried."

"It's more than that. You see… the problem is… I can't look at her or the baby. I can't stand to touch them. Whenever I'm near them, all I can think of is her strapped onto that table, her legs spread, screaming and this thing growing out of her; then the doctor rubbing her with his finger, and the scalpel, and the blood; cutting into her like she was some kind of animal. Not my wife. Nothing like her."

Frank placed a hand on Paul's shoulder. "It's OK. It's just something you're going through. It'll pass."

"It's been two weeks."

"Have you seen anyone? A doctor?"

"What's a doctor going to do for me? You think there's a pill they can give me for something like this?" There was a lot of anger in Paul's voice; and pain. Frank knew he shouldn't push things too far.

"I'm only saying it might be good to talk to someone. Professionally. Think about it." Frank pulled a business card out of his pocket that he had picked up from somewhere, and wrote a number on the back. He stuck the card in Paul's shirt pocket. "That's my home number. If you need to talk, call me. If you want me to go with you to see someone, or set something up... whatever — give me a shout. OK? Will you do that?"

Paul got up from his seat.

"OK?" Frank repeated.

"Yeah. Sure. Thanks." Paul struggled with his coat and Frank helped him into it.

"You're not driving, are you?"

"No. Cab."

"Fine. Remember what I said. The main thing is, don't worry. It's a phase. You'll get over it." He watched as Paul found his way out the door and into the street.

There was no light waiting for Paul when he arrived home. Not that he expected one. He was getting used to removing his shoes in the dark, then making his way up the stairs with the aid of the banister. He knew it was useless to try for a quiet entrance. His shoulder scraped against the wall and the floorboards squeaked. He'd have to use the bathroom. There was no getting around it, yet, at the top of the landing, he was on his tiptoes and moving toward the bedroom. He leaned his cheek against the door frame and listened.

"Is that you?" It was Karen, awake on the other side.

"Yeah. Who do you think?" Paul remembered when he used to say that as a joke. Those days were gone.

"Have you been drinking?"

"I went out for a few after work with the guys, yeah."

"I don't want you in here." There was no sound from Paul. "Do you hear me?"

"I hear you."

"Do you understand?"

Paul hung his head and spoke softly. "I understand." He dragged himself to the kitchen and poured a tall scotch. He opened the freezer door, leaned in, took a few ice cubes from a tray, dropped them into the glass and gave the drink a stir with his finger. I understand, he whispered. I understand. I don't understand, but, I understand.

He manoeuvred his way to the bathroom, put his drink on the toilet seat, began filling the tub. He dropped his clothes in a heap on the floor and climbed into the water. He picked up his drink and brought it to his lips. Steam condensed on the side of the glass; a couple of cold drops gathered at the bottom and fell onto his chest. He ignored them. He was busy watching the water rise over his legs, above his stomach, up to the middle of his ribs. He turned off the water, leaned back and drank. He thought how peaceful it was to soak in a hot bath. He could see his heart beating; could hear himself breathe. He thought how pleasant it must be, to simply sink below the surface and be filled with clean, warm water. Something else struck him. His head turned sharply to the pile of clothes. He leaned over and retrieved a business card from his shirt pocket. It read: ROY'S HOUSEPAINTING & DECORATING. There was an address and a phone number. Paul tried to figure out what he was doing with the card. Did the house need painting? Had he been talking to someone about it? Roy?

He rolled the card between his fingers. Something else suddenly struck him. A question: Is that you? The scotch was going to his head. He gave it a slight shake. He looked down and saw tiny bubbles form on the hairs of his legs. He sipped his drink. His whole body felt funny, like it was being taken over. He slid forward, dropped the card and watched the ripples it made. Is that you? Is that what she asked? Is that what she wanted to know? He wondered. The water was up to his chin.

A TRICK OF LIGHT

It was this last hour of work that Norman loved and hated the most, when the sun forced the darkness from its comfortable quarters and created the impression of glassy pools on the drying linoleum. He enjoyed these tricks of light but was unnerved at the ease with which his dim, secure world suddenly vanished. It signalled an end to solitude and the arrival of a noisy, bustling world he had difficulty comprehending and which, at times, frightened him. At the same time, there were certain attractions and even a desire to belong. He put away the mop and bucket and began polishing the office glass, erasing the prints and smudges which rose like guilty ghosts beneath the sun's bright interrogation. Behind his back the silence fell to the stamp of shoes, quick greetings and the hum of machinery. Smells of detergent were replaced by deodorant, perfume and the strong bouquet of Mr. Jennings' pipe tobacco.

"Good morning, Norman." Mr. Jennings didn't break stride as he snuffed the pipe with his thumb and tucked it into his jacket pocket.

"Good morning, Mr. Jennings." Norman didn't turn his head. He knew that if the two had ever met on the street, it was possible that they wouldn't recognize each other. Not that Norman cared. Everyone on the street appeared the same to him, anonymous and cold, so he avoided going out. He preferred to be alone; preferred the familiar, stationary shadows of his basement suite to the strange shadows that bumped mindlessly along the sidewalks; preferred the sounds of stray cats and leaky pipes to the din of shoppers and traffic. Loneliness was a constant friend, a companion; someone to cling to and depend on; someone who was strong but quiet. Very quiet. At times, perhaps, too quiet. So quiet that, occasionally, on certain nights when the dark was a little darker, the silence was a little more silent, it happened that Norman pulled the covers right over his head, curled up and cried.

"Hello, Norman." It was Rita. Lovely Rita with her thick auburn hair, green eyes and wide smile. Norman turned slightly in her direction. The sun played across Rita's teeth. She always said hello so easily, as though she meant it. As though it was important.

"Down boy." Betty leaned back in her chair as she spoke, allowing her skirt to rise above her knees. "You're drooling all over your nice, clean floor." Norman moved further along the wooden divider, his polishing spurred by the knowledge of being caught. He heard Betty's laugh joined by a few others. Had Rita seen him staring?

A few of the men gathered around the coffee machine. One of them, Pete Phillips, a large man with a loud voice, called out to Norman.

"Norm! C'mere! Yeah... come over here." Pete motioned with his hand and Norman walked over. "How ya doin', buddy? What's happening in the wide world of office maintenance, eh?"

Norman walked over, happy to put some distance between himself and the women. Pete wrapped an arm around his shoulders and pulled him into the group.

"Look at this, guys! Norm's got a spankin' new uniform and it looks real sharp on him." The men patted him on the back and pulled at his coveralls. "Yessir, that's a real smart outfit. And look at this." He spun Norman around. "They even put his name on the back."

"My n-n-name?"

"Sure. You mean you didn't know? No one told you?" Pete winked at the men and they laughed and whistled in agreement.

"N-n-no. I mean, I j-just got it." He twisted his neck to try and get a glimpse. "Wh-where?"

"Oh, you can't see it like that. It's in the middle. Big letters and plain as day. Two colours. Right guys?" They nodded and mumbled, oh yeah, sure, plain as day. "You'll have to wait till you take it off." The men continued shaking their heads in approval.

"Listen, Norm," Pete's voice became secretive as he leaned into

Norman's ear, "this would be a great chance to impress Rita. What do you think, guys?"

"Yeah. Absolutely." They responded in unison.

"What?" Norman tried to pull away but was muscled back into the circle.

"Now, come on... no need to be shy with us. We're your friends, eh? Everyone sees the way you look at her. We only want to help you out." There was no need to prompt the other men; they were into it and ready to urge Norman on to the next step.

"I d-d-don't know." He didn't like the idea of everyone being aware of his feelings toward Rita, yet he was struck by the possibility of speaking to her. Perhaps even impressing her in some small way. "What do I have to d-d-do?"

"Why, it's easy." Pete continued to do the talking. "I mean, she already says hello to you, right? You're not exactly total strangers."

"Y-yeah."

"'Course not. You're on a first-name basis. She calls you Norman and you call her Rita."

"I g-guess."

"So all you have to do is carry it one step further. You walk up, say hello like always, then ask her if she's noticed anything different about you. Before she answers, you turn around and show her your name on the back here and let her know that you're on your way up; that you won't always be a janitor; that you've got bigger plans."

The men could see that Norman wasn't entirely won over and they cut in with more support: "That's right. Easy. Go for it, Norm. What's to lose? Sure. Go tell her." Before he knew it, he'd been shuffled off and deposited in front of Rita's desk. He looked to the men to say something, but they were already back at the coffee machine. He was on his own.

"Hi, Ri-Ri-Ri..." He took a breath. "Ri-Rita."

"Hi, Norman. Are you finished for the day?"

"Well, yeah. Yeah, I'm d-done. I... I..." He noticed a crystal ornament on her desk, one of those cheap tourist things that snows on a country cottage when you shake it. "Th-that's very pretty."

"This? It's not, really. A friend gave it to me. As a joke." She picked the ornament up, shook it and held it to the light. The snow glittered as it fell. Norman watched and waited as the final snowflake settled. He didn't know what else to do, so he stood there. He felt like the tiny cottage trapped inside the glass. To free himself, he suddenly blurted out a few words, twisting his body around as he did so.

"Do you see? On my back? My n-n-name. I won't always be here. One d-d-day I'll be gone. G-g-gone. Do you see?"

"Yes." Rita's smile disappeared. Her voice went flat. "Yes. It's very nice. I'm sure you will, Norman." She covered the crystal with her palm.

"I won't always be a janitor, you know. I'm m-m-moving up. You know?" He stumbled away from the desk. "You know?"

"Yes. No. Of course you won't. Goodbye, Norman."

Norman raised a hand and waved awkwardly. "Bye. Bye, Rita." He fled toward the exit.

"Norman!" Dave Widley called to him.

"What?"

"What's that on your back?"

Norman put a hand on the back of his shoulder. "My n-n-name. They put my name on the back."

"That's what you were showing Rita?"

"Y-yeah. Why?"

"Because someone's played a trick on you." Dave peeled a sheet of paper from the uniform. Norman looked to the coffee area, but no one was there.

"Wh-what kind of trick?" He took the paper and read it slowly. The words and meaning were quite clear to him, but still, he spent a long time staring at it. His mouth hung open and his tongue worked in and out across his lower lip. He crumpled the note and stuffed it into his pocket. He didn't speak, simply dragged himself to the stairs and faded from view.

It was dark in Norman's basement apartment when he arrived. Raindrops struck the small row of windows and soon covered the glass with an oily film. He searched for the light switch, gave it a click and saw his room, his possessions, bared by the harsh glow of a single fixture. He shivered.

A towel draped the back of a wooden chair. Norman carefully folded it lengthwise and laid it snug along the bottom of the window. Through a dirty window pane he could make out the steel skeleton of another office tower sprouting from the ground. They're closing in, he thought. Burying me. He went into the kitchen and surveyed a row of canned soups and stews.

"Chicken noodle," he said aloud. "Chicken with rice." A thin smile formed on his lips. "Chicken vegetable." The words were emitted slowly with emphasis placed on individual syllables. "Chicken. Chee-kan. Chee-kan Gummm-booooh. Gum boo. Goo-boo!! Boo-boo!" He repeated himself again and again. He laughed forcibly, almost hysterically. "You boo-boo! You stupid boo-boo!" He pushed at the cans; fingered them; poked at them; rubbed their labels with his thumbs.

"You stupid! N-n-no w-w-wonder they laugh. No w-w-wonder." He grabbed a can and squeezed. "G-goddamn Chicken St-stew!" He choked on the words. His laughter turned to fits of coughing and wheezing. "G-g-goddamn!" He hiccupped. The can dropped heavily and struck the side of his ankle. He released a muffled scream. He tried to swear but the words couldn't get past the short breaths; the hiccups.

"G-g-g-... f-f-f-owww, ohhh!" His cheeks and chin were damp with tears and spit. His legs weakened and he staggered over to a deep cushioned armchair. He crawled in, tucked his legs beneath him and wrapped his face in his hands. It was several minutes before his breath calmed and his crying stopped. He wiped his eyes and nose with his shirt sleeve.

"It's no wonder they laugh. N-n-no w-wonder," he hiccupped. "I'm a joke. I've got no secrets. I've got nothing. I'm nothing." He rubbed his sore ankle and laughed. "Ow. I guess it's funny at that. It has to be. 'Cause if it wasn't; if it wasn't funny..." He attempted one of those smooth, ironic laughs used so often in the movies, but was sabotaged by another hiccup. "Ow! That hurts. I h-hurt. If it wasn't all so f-funny... If it wasn't all so f-funny... and if I d-didn't have you..." He reached for a framed picture on the side table. "No one knows about you. N-no one. My beautiful Rita. N-no one knows I have you here with me. To l-look at, talk to any time I want to. If it wasn't for you... I l-love you, Rita." He spoke to the picture; ran a finger lightly down Rita's cheek and gently kissed her on the mouth. "I love you." He clutched the picture to his chest, closed his eyes and drifted off to sleep.

It was not a restful night. Dreams returned Norman to that time when he'd made up his mind to steal the picture. He'd thought about it for weeks; had, in fact, been planning the theft from the first day it had materialized on Rita's desk. He had never stolen anything in his life. His upbringing had been strict. Not that he was religious. The question of God was too complicated for him, so he ignored it. His requirements were simpler and the Golden Rule provided as much guidance as he thought he needed. It wasn't right to take what wasn't yours, yet he knew that if he couldn't have Rita in the flesh, he had to have her photograph. Besides, a picture was no big deal. It didn't cost much and she could always have another made from the negative. He could even leave some money on the desk so it wouldn't exactly be stealing. All this he considered, but, in the long run, he decided not to leave money in case it led to too many questions. He worried that it would be his own honesty that would cause his undoing. Besides, who would know? He was the only one around for hours. As long as he removed it in the dark and had it hidden away by daybreak, he was safe. On the other hand, this very reason made him the perfect suspect. These questions troubled him, but he knew it would be infinitely worse if he refused to act.

"I love you, Rita. I love you." He talked in his sleep; his heart pounded; his body sweated; blood rushed to the tips of his fingers and caused them to tingle. His hands clenched. Breathing was short and shallow. His body trembled, shook; he gasped, then it was over. "I love you. Love you." She was his.

When Norman awoke, the clouds had parted and the sun was shining through the window. He leapt out of the armchair and checked the time. "Eight o'clock! I'm l-l-late. D-damn! Wh-what'll I t-tell Mr. Jennings? Wh-what if I get f-f-fired? And Rita? Wait. No traffic. N-no horns. It's Saturday. S-Saturday." He wiped his mouth with the back of his hand. "Th-that's right. Saturday." His head dropped and he noticed a few envelopes on the doormat. "J-junk mail," he said. "I g-guess I didn't see them last night. Who cares. More bills or 'Occupant'." He went into the kitchen, picked up the can from the floor and returned it to the shelf. Wait a second, he thought. His gaze fell again on the mail, then on the row of cans. He raised his hand and realized he was still holding Rita's picture. Her face stared back at him.

"Then again, one of those letters may be just what I've been waiting for. Wh-why n-not? Even thieves deserve a second chance. Even sh-sh-shadows. Even m-m-me."

Norman leaned his head into the office and knocked lightly. "Mr. Jennings? C-can I t-talk to you a m-m-minute?"

"Hm? Oh, Norman. I'm quite busy. What is it?"

"W-well, Mr. Jennings, I j-just w-wanted to tell you h-how m-m-much I appreciate all y-y-you've d-done for me. G-giving me a j-job and all." Norman's stutter was even worse than usual and he kept his eyes to the floor in order to keep his concentration.

"Yes, Norman. That's quite all right. You're doing a fine job." To try and avoid any further conversation, Mr. Jennings went back to his computer. Norman could sense the man's discomfort, but was determined to press ahead.

"That's wh-what I've c-c-come about, sir. I-I have to qu-quit. At the end of the w-week."

"Quit?" Mr. Jennings looked up from his keyboard. He hesitated a second. "Oh, so that's it. Well, I'm sorry, but there's no chance of giving you a raise at this point."

"Oh, no sir. I d-d-don't w-want a r-raise. It's just… I got a letter from my uncle in Alberta."

"Your uncle? Well, if he's sick or something I'm sure we can work out some time off without you having to quit."

"You d-don't understand. He-he's dead."

"Dead? Oh, I'm sorry to hear that. Still, there's no reason to quit on us now, is there?"

"H-h-he l-left me some m-money."

"Even so, it takes quite a bit of money to get you through these days. You're still a young man. Plenty of years ahead of you."

"A l-lot of m-money, really."

"A lot of money?"

"Oh, yes." Norman could tell that the issue of money had grabbed Mr. Jennings' attention, so he proceeded with more confidence. After all, he thought, in for a dime, in for a dollar. "He was a v-very rich m-man. Oil."

"Oil? Tell me, Norman — how much, exactly, are you getting?"

"The l-letter didn't say exactly," he hedged.

"Oh." There was disappointment in the man's voice and perhaps a sense of doubt. Norman jumped back in with both feet.

"A f-few m-million anyway, they figure."

"A few million!" Mr. Jennings smiled. He rose from his chair and approached Norman. "A few million, you say? Well, well. And what do you plan to do with all this new-found wealth?"

"I g-guess I haven't had much time to th-think about it, my uncle just being dead and everything."

"Of course. Sad thing about your uncle, but life goes on, right? Nothing else to be done."

"Yes, sir. Travel, maybe."

"Hm? Oh, yes — travel. A splendid idea. In the future." He stressed these last words and placed an almost fatherly hand on Norman's shoulder. "In the future. But first, you must think about the present. Without a secure present you have no future. Put your money where it will work for you and then go out and spend a bit on some foolishness. Travel? I have some friends who would be very interested in advising you; in helping you through this transition period. Why don't we get together for lunch this week and discuss it? My treat, of course. Any place you want. I'll invite these friends of mine. You'll like them. I'll call them now. We'll talk." As Mr. Jennings moved toward the phone Norman began to back out of the office. "Don't forget now! I'll set a date and time and let you know. One thing you'll learn, my boy, is that there's no such thing as too many friends or too much money. Think of me as your friend, Norman. We'll do lunch. Talk. Remember, my treat."

Norman's status changed immediately. News of his inheritance had travelled through the office like a plague of invisible locusts, affecting everyone and everything it touched. Pete apologized for last week's 'prank' and Norman graciously forgave him. He even insisted on buying Norman a coffee and danish as a small gesture of his friendship. There was suddenly no end of friends, not the least surprise being Betty. She followed him around like a stray cat — a very affectionate stray cat — pressing her body against his; purring questions in his ear.

"What do you plan to do with all your money, Norman?"

"I don't know. Travel, maybe."

"I've always wanted to travel. Spain. France. Greece. Hawaii. I've never had the money, though. Or anyone to travel with." Betty had the uncanny ability of being able to transform her eyes from two drab lumps of mud into the most dazzling jewels depending on who she was talking to and what she was after. The stakes were obviously high. No stars shone brighter than when she was around Norman.

"N-no," answered Norman. "It wouldn't be much fun to travel alone." Betty was nice. Norman knew that she was only after his money, but he was enjoying the attention. He liked having her around. She was pretty and could carry on a conversation all by herself. He didn't have to do or say anything; just sit back, relax and let things happen. The problem was, he still wanted Rita and she practically ignored him.

Norman waited until Friday, his final day on the job, before he approached Rita. He was afraid it might turn out like last week; that he'd simply be a bumbling bag of knots, unable to express himself in words. He was surprised that he could even walk properly, yet as he neared her desk, he felt a strange sort of confidence. He smiled and brushed an imaginary hair from his forehead.

"Hello, Rita."

"Hello, Norman." She stopped typing and glanced up. Norman was wearing a new, navy blue suit, light pink shirt and a blue tie with tiny red dots. The tie was held in place with a bowling pin tie clip. Norman's hair was cut and styled. "You look very nice," she said. "Very dapper."

"Yes. Thank you. B-Betty helped me shop. She p-put everything together."

"She has good taste."

"The tie clip's mine. B-Betty doesn't l-like it."

"I'm sure it'll be a big hit in Alberta." They both laughed. "We'll hardly know what to do around here without you."

"Y-yeah. Th-that's what I w-wanted to t-talk to you about." He played with the tie clip. "I... I... w-w-want you to c-come with me, R-Rita."

"What?"

"C-come with me. I love you." He covered one of her hands with both of his own. "Y-you don't have to m-marry me. Just c-come with me. I'll treat you g-good and if it doesn't w-work out, you can l-leave any time. I w-won't try and stop you." He kept his hands on hers as he stammered out the words. "I kn-know I'm not handsome or anything, but I'm n-not u-ugly. And I'm n-not st-stupid even though... even th-though... I'm slower, that's all. It t-takes m-me longer s-sometimes."

"Don't, Norman," she stopped him. "You don't need to tell me this. I know and I understand and I'm flattered that you... like me..."

"I love you."

"That you love me. But I can't go away with you. It isn't possible."

"You d-don't love me."

"I like you, but, no, I don't love you. We're friends."

"I want to b-be more than friends. You might learn to l-love me. In time."

"Norman, there's someone else. I'm in love with another man."

"Another man?" He stared at her. "Another man? I n-never thought of that. Wh-why didn't I think of that? I mean, why wouldn't you? I guess I am st-stupid."

"You're not stupid. How could you know? We never talk except to say good morning."

"I sh-should have kn-known though. Who is he?"

"Just a man. You don't know him. He doesn't work here." She removed her hand from Norman's and pointed to the glass ornament. "He's the one who gave me this."

"You love him?"

"Yes."
"And he l-loves you?"
"Yes."
"And you and I... are f-friends?"
"Yes."
"Then I suppose I should give this b-back to you." He pulled a package from inside his jacket and handed it to Rita. She opened it.
"My picture. You took it?"
"I'm s-sorry. I'm a thief and a l-l-liar."
"If you had asked I'd've given it to you."
"I was too afraid."
"Why don't you take it with you? As a gift."
"N-no. Th-thanks. I d-don't need it now. Now, we're friends." He extended his hand. Rita took it and they squeezed softly. Norman released her and picked up the ornament. "It's a silly thing, really. Isn't it?" He shook it and watched the snow settle.
"Yes. But the light plays tricks with the snowflakes. See how they change colour?"
"Yes." He put the ornament down. "Goodbye, Rita." Norman turned and saw that a crowd had gathered between him and the door. He smiled and walked toward them. The men shook his hand and slapped his back. Everyone congratulated him and wished him luck. Betty leaned in and kissed his cheek.
"Remember, if you ever get lonely, give me a call," she said. "I wrote my number inside your shirt cuff."
"G-g-goodbye. Goodbye." Norman waved and entered the hallway. No one stopped waving and shouting until he was out of sight, then there was a brief silence. The crowd shrugged and dispersed. Good old Norm, someone said. What a lucky stiff, said another. He won't know what to do with it all. The remarks reduced to whispers. Dave Widley stood by Rita's desk.
"Do you really think he had an uncle in Alberta? A rich uncle?" asked Rita.
"Who knows?" Dave took the ornament in his hand and shook it. "Kind of a foolish trick just to gain some attention. And costly, too. Where did you get this?"
"I bought it. At a garage sale. Do you like it?"

"No. Not really. Do you?" He shook it again.

"I'm not sure. I bought it as a lark. No one likes it, but it seems to attract a lot of attention. I don't know what it is about it. Hold it up. The light plays tricks. See how the snowflakes change colour? They almost burn. See?"

THE REGULAR

Him again. Again him. Sometimes three or four times a day. Sometimes more. He calls himself a regular and tells us we are lucky to have him as a customer. He could take his business elsewhere. We wish he would, my wife and I. He's a regular all right, but what business? Oh yes, once in awhile he buys a package of cigarettes. Or, oh yes, a chocolate bar. That's it. And even this (we're sure), only so he can claim to be a regular without danger of reproach. My wife calls me a coward. 'You're a coward,' she says. 'You let him boss you around in your own store.' I tell her we must be tactful; that we're new here; that I'm doing my best. She won't be soothed. I tell him (this regular customer) that the situation is impossible. I try to reason with him. I say, 'What if all our regular customers (our true regular customers) behaved in a similar fashion? We would be unable to stay in business; we'd go bankrupt in a month. Less than a month.' I try to explain logically. He only fumes. His eyebrows rise, his lips turn down at the corners, he regards me with great indignation. 'Listen to me,' he says, 'you slant-eyed little chink...' He chooses always to address me this way, as you slant-eyed little chink. Bad enough he insults me with racial slurs, but he is barely taller than myself, except he is much stockier, more heavily built and much stronger. He snaps apples in half with his bare hands; he cracks pecan nuts between his fingers. Which brings me to the source of my (our) distress — the man wanders among the racks of fruits, nuts and vegetables helping himself to large samplings which he has no intention of paying for, just as he has no intention of buying anything else (except, oh yes, once in a long while, the cigarettes or chocolate bar). I glare at him from the counter; I cough loudly hoping that he will take the hint. He doesn't. Finally I must approach him. I am very civil, I think. I again tell him the situation is impossible. We cannot afford, et cetera. 'Listen to me,' he says, 'you slant-eyed...' It never changes. 'I'm a regular customer,' he repeats. 'With the amount you mark stuff up you can afford...' He goes on like this, raising his voice until the other customers can't stand it any longer and they leave. Meanwhile, you understand, we know (my wife and I), that he shops at the large supermarket where the produce is not as fresh and the prices are much higher, but, as my wife says, it's run by white people. So he continues his methods of fear and intimidation in order to feast on grapes, cherries, apricots, apples, pecans (I wouldn't be surprised, one day, to find him devouring an entire watermelon, having broken the tough rind across his knee and scooping out the contents with a tongue shaped very much like a long, deep spoon, and then what would I do?) while our little business falls to ruin. He ends all of this with a hearty laugh, of course, and calls me his friend. I'm not happy with the situation, but, what can I do? Call the police? How would the other customers react? And what about the revenge (and needless to say, he would seek revenge) that we would face? I explain this all to my wife, but to no avail. She stamps her foot. She raises the machete, points it at me, takes a large swipe at the air, then brings it down — CHOP! — to trim the spoiled ends of yesterday's romaine. She chews the inside of her lip. She refuses to believe there is nothing to be done. The machete again — CHOP! 'Next time,' she says. 'Next time, we see.' Well, next time is here and my wife has spotted him near the cherries. As I hope I've made clear, there is nothing covert about the man's actions. He is open and deliberate in his (let's face it) thievery. I see my wife closing in, like a cat upon its prey. Should I attempt to interfere? After all, there are considerations, right? Legal matters? As well as... what? Codes of ethics? But what about him? What about his behaviour? No. Perhaps it's for the best. Once out of jail, move to another city, a smaller town, we can... but the bird has taken the bait, the ripe fruit being carried toward a pair of parted lips, almost there, when, suddenly, my wife springs and (I can't look) — CHOP! I uncover my eyes in time to see segments of fingers drop to the floor and bounce among great spheres of ruby-red blood. But no, not fingers and not blood. Merely the hacked ends of a bunch of carrots mingled with the spilled cherries. The man's mouth is gaping, as if he is about to speak; about to launch into his (by now) memorized routine, when — CHOP! Another scattering of carrot sections as the machete edges dangerously close to the man's immobile hand. Then the machete raises a third time, but before my wife has a chance to test its true sharpness, the man, white as a sheet, turns tail and runs. The blade whistles through the empty air. My wife watches the man's retreat until he vanishes around a corner. She looks at me and releases a short blast of air from her nostrils. Then she spits on the floor, turns and goes back to her wooden carving board. She places a sweet cantaloupe on the board, raises the machete and brings it down, stopping a hair's width from the rough skin. She looks at me. She grins. She laughs. I laugh. We laugh. We laugh and laugh.

RESTLESS AND FLEETING

Mike had been out. Now that he was home he marched straight into the kitchen. Laura was sitting at the table with a cup of coffee, reading a book. Mike didn't hesitate, just slipped up close behind her and began kissing the back of her neck.

"Watchya readin'?" he asked.

"Virginia Woolf," she said.

"You know, that shit fucks up your head."

"Yeah?" She smiled, enjoying the attention being paid to her neck and shoulders.

"Yeah. Literature." He said the word with distaste. "It oughta be banned. You start with Virginia Woolf and next thing you know you're into Gertrude Stein. It's a vicious circle. Pretty soon you're walking around with stones in your pockets mumbling things like, 'A day is a day. Every day is a day. Each day is a day. Each and every day is a day,' and so on and so forth. There's no getting around it. You're lost. Friends and loved ones try to reason with you but it's too late. Finally, they have to lock you up for your own protection. It's sad." Mike knew a thing or two. He'd been to university, got a BA, which meant (as he was fond of saying) — bugger all, since it never amounted to getting him a job. Still, he liked books — "good" books — and was recognized as containing a veritable well of almost useless information. On the other hand, he could be great fun at parties, if he was in the mood.

"Really?"

"Oh, sure." Mike ran a hand under Laura's sweater and bra. He gave her nipple a gentle squeeze.

"You have some idea to save me?"

"I was thinking of a quickie." He got her to her feet without the book and lifted the sweater off over her head.

"You just had it this morning," she grinned.

"Yeah, well — this morning was this morning and now is now."

"Was that Gertrude Stein as well?"

It was one of those rare Saturdays they had off together. They had no kids. They weren't expecting company. They let their clothes drop in the hall on the way to the bedroom.

Laura had her body pressed against Mike's, her arm curved casually across his chest.

"So, what's got into you today?"

"Hm? Oh, nothing. You know — just restless, I guess."

"Restless? What does that mean?" She removed her arm.

"Restless, that's all." He climbed out of bed and stood in front of the dresser mirror.

"About what?"

"Nothing. You know. The usual. Fucking job, fucking this-and-that, fucking weather."

"You're not getting any ideas, are you?" Laura raised herself up on her elbows.

"Ideas? What are you talking about? What sort of ideas?"

"You know." She fluffed up her pillow and stuck it behind her head. She did the same with Mike's and pulled up the sheet to cover her breasts.

"Are you crazy? I was practically a kid when I went through all that."

"The last time wasn't so long ago."

"All right, I was acting like a kid. Don't worry. The job's fine. I never thought I'd end up selling fucking appliances at fucking Sears, but there you go."

"You were lucky to get that job."

"Let's drop it, OK? I'm not thinking about going out on a tear. I'm not thinking about quitting my job. Things are good, right? We're both working. We've got a nice house. We've got money in the bank. We're insured up to our eyeballs. We've got it made, right?"

"You're not the only one, you know. I get bored with my job, too. It's just..."

"I know, I know. Let's drop it, OK? Everything's fine."

Laura had worked for the same insurance company for a dozen or so years, while Mike had spent most of his time bouncing from job to job. The three years he'd been with Sears was the longest he'd stayed at anything. The other jobs had all ended the same way. Mike would say that he was bored, that the job was going nowhere, that he wasn't getting paid what he deserved. He'd start swearing more and drinking more; he'd begin to pick fights with the employees, the bosses. Then one day he'd up and quit. Tell them to shove their job up their ass. That was his way. The funny thing was, no matter what job he took, he was good at it and people liked him. At the beginning. Laura too would hardly complain. It was kind of exciting. Besides, Mike always managed to find another job in pretty short order. He couldn't be accused of being lazy, that was sure. But the novelty had worn thin over the years. She wanted security. She was tired of having to make new friends every time Mike flew off the handle and needed a change. Times were not the same as they once were; jobs were scarce and Mike wasn't getting any younger. Neither of them were. She was happy with her life, now; with her friends.

Mike leaned into the mirror, pulling at his face, gazing into his eyes, examining his tongue and teeth. He straightened and showed his profile to the glass. He stuck out his chest and sucked in his gut. Laura chewed the corner of a fingernail, watching him.

"Whatchya think? Am I getting too fat?" He let out his breath and smacked his belly.

"You've put on a few pounds. Not much. Nothing to worry about."

"Yeah. Pretty solid still for a guy my age."

"A guy your age?"

"Sure. In two years I'm going to be forty. In twelve years, I'll be fifty."

"Yeah. And in twenty-two years you'll be sixty."

"Sixty?" He turned to check his butt. "Y'know, when I was a teenager, none of us ever expected to reach twenty-five. We knew we were all either going to die in a nuclear war or else be killed driving drunk in a car crash. Now everyone figures they're going to stay young and beautiful forever. Why the change, eh? I mean, the world's just as fucked as it ever was — maybe more. There's genocide going on in eastern Europe. You can't swim in the lake or walk in the sun. The sky is fucking falling all around us. Where's the logic?"

"Is that what's bothering you? That you're getting old?"

"Nah. I'm just running off at the mouth." He crossed to her and kissed her on the lips. "I told you. It's the weather. The winters are too long in this city. Look, I'm going to clean up and go meet Phil for a couple games of pool." He headed to the bathroom.

"I thought that's where you were this morning?"

"There was a message waiting for me he couldn't make it till later. I sat around drinking coffee, grabbed some lunch, checked out the music stores. I was going to kill time waiting around but I came home, right? Like I said, restless."

"What do you want to do about dinner?"

"Why don't you pick out a video and we'll order Chinese. I'll get a bottle of wine."

"Anything in particular?"

"You choose. Maybe something foreign. You know — sexy, but with some intelligence. My brain's getting numb from talking about goddamn fridges and stoves and fucking microwave ovens." Mike threw on a clean sweatshirt, slipped into his underwear and jeans, picked up his socks and shoes in the hall and called back as he left, "I won't be late."

Laura heard the door close and shook her head.

"A day is a day," she whispered. "A day is a day is…" She got up and went to the bathroom.

When Mike entered the pool hall he saw Phil at a table by himself racking a set of snooker balls.

"You been here long?" asked Mike.

"A while. Figured as long as I was supposed to be shooting pool with you all day I might as well come in early, just in case. How'd it go?" Phil poked Mike's ribs with the tip of his cue.

"It didn't. She told me she's getting back together with her husband." Mike searched out a second cue and rolled it across the felt to see if it was straight.

"What? You mean the guy who slaps her around and tells her she's too ugly and stupid to find someone else?"

"That's him. Seems he's changed. He wants her back. They've worked things out."

"Right."

"That's what I said. Anyway, she says he loves her and she loves him and everything's going to be different this time. Tells me she wants to be faithful. Tells me I should do the same. Tells me there's nothing more beautiful than an honest and trusting relationship." Mike broke and sent the balls crashing in all directions. Nothing dropped.

"Same old bullshit. It's like someone who gives up cigarettes. Or booze. Or discovers God. They become converts and start preaching like things have never been any different or any better. They've seen the light; they've been purified. Meanwhile, six months, maybe a year later, the bottom falls out. 'Course, by then, nothing's the same. You can't go back. Anything you ever had that was maybe, outside, is over." Phil sank a red, the pink and another red. He circled the table, checking shape on the blue. He dropped it. "Thirteen," he said.

"That's what I told her."

"What did you say she was? Twenty-seven? Twenty-eight?" He dropped another red. "Fourteen."

"Twenty-seven."

"With two young kids, right?" He set up on the blue again and sank it. "Nineteen."

"Yeah. You gonna let me play, or what?"

"And you weren't thinking of leaving Laura, right?"

"No. I love Laura. We've got a life together."

"Then it's for the best." A red ball chased around the pocket then rolled against the rag. "Shit." Phil leaned against his cue. "I mean, look at the bright side. You spent a couple of months flirting, you had some laughs, a few drinks, you screwed a couple of times — now it's over. No one the wiser and no one hurt. You're lucky."

"Yeah, still..." Mike surveyed the table. "You left me absolute dick."

"Still, what? Take it as a gift. Who else do you know's been screwin' a chick ten years younger, eh?"

"Now that's the point, y'see." Mike looked up from the table. "It was more than that. We had something. There was some kind of, I don't know, energy that happened between us. A kind of... connection. It was like we were fated, like our two histories were determined, in some way, to overlap. You know, everything else apart — age, marriage, kids — whatever." He shot into a cluster of reds and watched them scatter. He waited for one of them to drop, but none did.

"C'mon. You been married almost ten years, right? And she's split from a guy who... who didn't treat her too well, right? You were both looking for a change. You wanted to see if the grass was greener and she wanted to feel like she was attractive."

"You got a quarter?"

"What for?"

"I need to call her."

"Jeezus, Mike. You know what you're doing? You're looking for that one last time. Except there ain't no one last time. Let it drop."

"That's not what it is. I mean, yeah, I'm sad that it's over and, yeah, the sex was great, but, that's not what it is. What it is, is the way it ended. Her being so fucking formal about the whole thing; so practical. As though we hadn't shared something that was personal; something that was between us and had nothing to do with anyone or anything else. I mean, like, when we were together, we were kids again. Everything felt clean and innocent and exciting."

"It's impossible, pal. What you're talking about is books and movies, not real life. I mean, what's it going to get her in the long run, eh? Hanging around with you? At least with her ex, she knows where she stands; she knows what she's in for."

"You got a quarter or no?"

"Nuts. You're nuts. Here." Phil flipped a coin in Mike's direction, gave his head a shake then went back to the table. He banged in a red ball, sank the black, made a combination on the next red and set up on the black again. Mike returned.

"Well?"

"No answer." He placed the quarter on the table edge.

"There you go. It's written in the stars." He pocketed the black. "I mean, what were you going to say anyway? You probably don't even know."

"Is it my shot?" Mike picked up his cue as Phil replaced the black to its spot. Phil looked at the ball and shrugged.

"Sure. Why not. You couldn't hit shit with a shovel anyhow." Mike went after a red and missed. "Did you know what you were going to say? Huh?"

"Yeah, I knew."

"Uh-huh? What?"

Mike went after another red. Then the yellow ball. Then the blue and another red. He never came close. Phil stood watching. He placed a hand on Mike's shoulder. Mike released the cue and looked up at Phil.

"What's going on, eh? C'mon, tell me."

"I… I was going to tell her…" Mike straightened and stared past Phil's ear. Phil wasn't sure if Mike was going to break into tears or start tearing the joint apart. "I was going to ask her…"

"What? What were you going to ask her? C'mon. I'm sorry I was sounding off. I was being an asshole. I'm sorry. I didn't know. What were you going to ask her? I'm listening."

"I was going to ask her… to say something nice to me." Mike stopped there. Phil didn't know whether to jump in or just wait. Finally, he spoke.

"Like what? What did you want her to say?"

"I don't know. Something. I mean, I know that what's happened is probably for the best; that it couldn't have gone on forever between us, but, it's like, the memory… I want the memory to be of the good times we had. I want to know that, even though it's over, she cared and it meant something to her. I want to know that… I don't know. I just… I can't have it end this way. Cold. Distant."

"Come on. Let's pack up. We'll go somewhere, I'll buy you a beer." Phil cleared the table and grabbed their coats. "You know your problem? You're a romantic. You read all the wrong books. You keep thinking that life is something you have some control over. In fact, no one has any control. We're fucked from the start. All of us. The world is fucked. That's just the way it is. There's no escaping it. Best thing is to have a couple of beers and forget about it." Phil guided Mike by the arm toward the door and they left.

"You made it." Laura was stretched out on the couch.

"It's not late, is it?"

"Not very. Eight."

"Phil and I went for a few beers. I almost forgot the wine." Mike tossed his coat on a hook and wandered into the kitchen. He opened the wine and poured two glasses. "You get a flick?"

"Mm. Spanish. *Women on the Verge of a Nervous Breakdown*." Mike placed the glasses on the table. "It's supposed to be a comedy."

"Uh-huh. I'll be back." He walked to the bathroom. Laura watched and saw him stagger slightly. Not much. Slightly. She heard the toilet flush and the water running in the sink. Mike washed his hands and face; he stared into the mirror. He pulled at his cheeks, his jaw. He patted under his chin with the back of his hand. He dried himself, then joined Laura on the couch. They sipped their wine in silence. Both seemed as if they were about to speak, but neither did for a long while. They just sat there, sipping their wine and staring in front of them.

"Can I ask you something?" It was Mike who spoke.

"Sure. What?" Laura didn't turn.

"Would you do something for me?"

The two were sitting next to each other. Mike took Laura's hand in his; she faced him. She thought that Mike looked suddenly quite serious. She thought that she had seen this look before.

"What is it?" she asked. "Are you all right?" She felt frightened — not of Mike, not physically, at any rate. The fear was more to do with her; something about her, perhaps a certain idea or emotion she figured as long since dead and buried that now seemed to be rising up inside her.

"I want you to tell me something."

"Tell you what?"

"I don't know. Something. Anything." His voice quivered. He allowed his head to slip down into her lap. He squeezed his eyes shut.

"What do you want me to tell you?" She repeated herself, not knowing what else to say. What could she tell him, she wondered? That at this moment all she wanted was to lash out at him; beat him with her fists; scratch his eyes and face? Tell him that, more than anything else in the world, and for no good reason she could put her finger on, she wanted to hurt him; see him suffer? No, she thought. There was nothing she could tell him. Not now. Not with him like this, in her lap. Not with her like this, knowing that once she began, she'd be unable to stop herself. She put her hand on his head and held it there. She clenched her mouth and stared across the room, into the shadows. A day is a day, she thought. Each and every day is a day. They remained like that, the two of them, almost frozen within the harsh glow of the table lamp, unable to speak, barely able to breathe. Waiting.

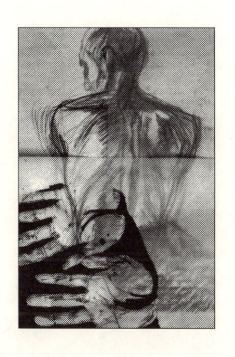

PASSENGERS

He does not stand out in a crowd. A man of business, he has been tailor-made to fit his uniform: blue, three-piece suit, red tie, black shoes; the gleaming white shirt has a starched collar. It has been long enough so that he appears almost comfortable, yet there is some affectation in his movements which suggests that he is only a passenger and it is his outfit that controls speed and direction. The man is, in fact, a hindrance to the mobility and natural ease of the suit. He pokes his head through the stiff collar as if through the window of a bus. The suit complains bitterly at the added wind resistance and would prefer to drop the man off at the first stop. Instead, the shoes pinch, the collar scrapes and the buttons on the vest tighten. The man coughs slightly at the discomfort and contemplates dieting.

He moves along the sidewalk; his mind is neither on his moving nor on the sidewalk. Rather, it resides in the briefcase which is pressed tight against his ribs with his right elbow. His left hand grips the forward, top edge of the case while a right hand maintains a hold on the forward, lower edge. There is such an atmosphere of determination and attention given to secure the case that one could mistake it for the rudder of a ship guiding the man through a storm-pitched sea. Perhaps it *is* a rudder, after all, for it seems obvious that without it the man would surely do himself some damage by tripping over a dog, walking smack into a mailbox or wandering lost in front of a speeding taxi. How he notices the slip of paper lying on the ground ahead of him cannot be determined. It somehow catches his eye and arrests his motion. His clothes flatten against the back of his body, his briefcase bucks beneath his arm, the ticking of his watch pierces his wrist like the needle of a sewing machine. A fragile wind skips the paper closer to his feet. He bends, picks up the paper, unfolds it and reads. There is an address: #309 - 723 - 4th Ave., and a time: 9 a.m. He checks his watch: 8:50 a.m. The address is just minutes away. There is time. He stares vacantly past the slip of paper while continuing to clench the leather case. The case twists and strains like a perverse divining rod. He bites his lip and makes a hissing sound through his teeth. He crushes the note and crosses toward a garbage can. He pauses. Looks left, right, forward, back, up and down. He checks his watch: 8:52. There is time. His eyes pass from the briefcase to the note, from the note to the briefcase. If he hurries. If he hurries there is time. He removes the lid from the container. The briefcase growls, spits, scratches at the man's bare hands as it's tossed in with the other refuse. The lid is replaced, the note is buried in a coat pocket, and the man turns, walks briskly to Fourth Avenue. The suit struggles for a moment, tries to trip him, then surrenders to the change of events.

At the stairs to the apartment block, the man again pauses, compares the address on the building with that on the note. Satisfied, he enters and takes the elevator to the third floor. It is 8:56. He discovers the door to room 309 unlocked, so he walks inside. The room is empty except for furniture which backs against the wall under the man's steady gaze. The room is quiet except for the low chatter of clothing and bed sheets. On a table next to the telephone is a revolver. The man picks it up and it feels comfortable in his grip; his index finger curls naturally around the trigger, the weight is neither too heavy nor too light. He scratches his chin with the silencer and grins. Behind him, there is the click of a door handle turning. He spins, crouches like a polished assassin and fires four bullets into the body of a man who collapses face down on the carpet. It is 9 a.m. The killer kneels and removes a small note from the dead man's fist. There is a message: *I've been waiting for you*, and an address: #704 - 1842 Rimmer St. There is also a time: 11 a.m. He cleans the handle of the revolver with a handkerchief, replaces it beside the phone and exits. Through the hallway he takes long, confident strides. He is calm. He breathes easily, fully, feels his chest expand and contract. His eyes gather in the ivory colour of the walls, the rich braided texture of the carpet, the sparkle of the brass buttons in the upholstered elevator. In the street, he loosens his collar, removes his tie, undoes his vest. He casts away his coat, shoes and socks, and skips along the sidewalk, smiling, singing, shouting, his heart pounding, his blood rushing, his lungs pumping new air into his chest, stomach, arms, legs and head. He rips open his shirt, allowing the wind to tickle the hairs on his belly. The sky is blue. The concrete is hard. The traffic is deafening. There is movement and life all around, and at an address on Rimmer Street, a person waits patiently, like a passenger at a station, for the arrival of the 11 o'clock train and a one-way ticket out.

DRESS REHEARSAL

The room is square and windowless. White prevails: white ceramic floor, white plastic walls, white ceiling. Only the presence of fluorescent lighting allows for a faint blue glow to emanate from the otherwise pale and antiseptic setting.

A single door blemishes one white wall and opposite this, off-centre, near the back corner of the room, a rectangular table is situated surrounded by ten figures, four on each side and one at either end. The conversation appears casual. There are no papers or pens to suggest a business meeting. Elbows rest on the pale arborite, hands support chins, stroke beards or simply stir the air. An odd head occasionally turns and glances about the room. There is no semblance of order, no items which might indicate leadership — neither itinerary, nor special seat, nor gavel. Except for the table, ten chairs and ten figures, the room is bare and, to disturb the silence, the murmur of a fan and ten voices — calm, dim, textureless — voices as might be heard in any waiting room, mingling with the air, clinging to the ceiling, unable to generate enough substance to form a shadow.

When the door splinters, so the calm glass of the room shatters. Words, half-words, melt down the corners of mouths. Blood pumps, igniting cheeks and foreheads. Pores steam open, flesh dissolves; muscles, tendons tingle and jump spasmodically. Every head twists toward the door. All eyes report the entry of four men who place themselves strategically between the table and the open door. Revolvers raise, fix at eye-level; gloved fingers squeeze. Figures at the table collapse as breath escapes through tiny holes drilled in throats and foreheads. Others attempt to flee but only succeed in allowing bullets to penetrate temples, spines, chests, bellies. One figure covers his face with his arms. A bullet shatters his forearm, bone fragments explode into his cheeks and eyes. The next shot pierces his heart. Two others manage to overturn the table and use it as a shield, a battering ram, to attack, but bullets cut through and bluntly strike or else carve the soft wood into a barrage of deadly spears and arrows, felling the two in mid-charge, dropping them like inadequate bison. Another figure, wounded, takes advantage of the diversion, the slight attention paid to the charging table, to stumble toward the group huddled by the door, to raise his arms above his head, to remain standing long enough to plunge the sharpened end of a split wooden chair leg into the surprised chest of one assassin before the butt of a rifle efficiently crushes his skull and ends his death-dealing.

Of the four who entered, three are left to stand together and silently survey the bloody scene. One checks his watch, scribbles something in a notepad. A second gazes down at his dead comrade, grunts, then returns his attention to the group. The three face each other, shake their heads, slap shoulders and exit.

The room is square and windowless. White prevails: white ceramic floor, white plastic walls, white ceiling. Only the presence of fluorescent lighting allows for a faint blue glow to emanate from the otherwise pale and antiseptic setting.

A single door blemishes one white wall and opposite this, off-centre, near the back corner of the room, a rectangular table is situated surrounded by ten figures, four on each side and one at either end. The conversation appears casual. There are no papers or pens to suggest a business meeting. Elbows rest on the pale arborite, hands support chins, stroke beards or simply stir the air. An odd head occasionally turns and glances about the room. There is no semblance of order, no items which might indicate leadership — neither itinerary, nor special seat, nor gavel. Except for the table, ten chairs and ten figures the room is bare and, to disturb the silence, the murmur of a fan and ten voices — calm, dim, textureless — voices as might be heard in any waiting room, mingling with the air, clinging to the ceiling, unable to generate enough substance to form a shadow.

When the door splinters, so the calm glass of the room shatters. Words, half-words, melt down the corners of mouths. Blood pumps, igniting cheeks and foreheads. Pores steam open, flesh dissolves; muscles, tendons dangle and jump spasmodically. Every head twists toward the door. All eyes report the entry of four men who place themselves strategically between the table and the open door. Revolvers raise, fix at eye level; gloved fingers squeeze. Figures at the table collapse as breath escapes through tiny holes drilled in throats and foreheads. Others are blown backward against the wall, their ribcages torn apart, impacted with lead. Streaks of red trace their descent on the white-plastic walls, their bodies blood-sliding to the floor. One mammoth figure refuses to fall under the hail of bullets, lunging at the attackers like a wounded mastodon, chest raging crimson, shoulder-length blonde hair and beard drenched and dripping red. His arms form tusks aimed at the throat of one crouched gunman, the fingers pointed, the nails hard and sharp as carved ivory, his entire body and movement centring upon one action — impalement. Revolvers continue to fire into the now dead beast, this giant who blindly rolls like a tidal wave toward a beach, the momentum of his massive frame still threatening to crush, drown or suffocate the crouched marksman. They aim at his legs, whittle him down until he drops under the weight of his own body. Power-spent, he tumbles and rolls forward, a gentle wash, barely touching the foot of the gunman who has not budged except to fire into this ton of maddened flesh, now motionless, save for the blood; the blood foaming, bubbling from numberless holes, oozing thick as satin and covering him in a mantle of scarlet.

The four stand erect. Unmoving. No one speaks, merely scan the room, check watches, scribble a few marks in a notepad, then exit.

The room is square and windowless. White prevails: white ceramic floor, white plastic walls, white ceiling. Only the presence of fluorescent lighting allows for a faint blue glow to emanate from the otherwise pale and antiseptic setting.

A single door blemishes one wall and it hangs open, the wood split and shattered, as if forced by heavy boots. Four men enter the room. They wear white smocks and carry various pieces of equipment: pens, clipboards, camera, assorted measuring devices. The man who operates the camera snaps open the leather case and raises the lens to eye level. He sets to work photographing the area, beginning with general shots of figures positioned nearest the table. Next, he divides the area visually into four sections, pans right to left, concentrating on details regarding figure posture and placement. He then enters each quadrant in turn, crouches over individual figures, isolates the various sections of the bodies, focussing separately on facial expressions, twists of necks, bends in arms, hands and fingers, curvature of torsos, crooks in legs and feet. Moving slowly, methodically through the grid, the camera's attention shifts, finally, to one fallen figure who had managed to separate from the others. The camera hovers over, circling like a fat vulture, curiously clicking back view, side view, front, then swoops backward in order to secure a perspective capable of illustrating the distance between the prostrate figure and the table.

As the camera busily clicks, a second man handles a measuring tape and calculates distances: table to chairs, chairs to figures, table to figures, figure to figure, soberly noting the dimensions and recording them on a lined form. At one point, he pauses, regards the massive figure pinned flat to the floor, looks back to the table, then to the figure, shakes his head, makes a mental calculation, scribbles a brief note and continues measuring.

A third man meticulously examines each body for bullet holes, totalling their number and recording them on a blue form. In his right hand he clutches the clipboard and pen. In his left hand he holds a stiff, 1 1/2" paintbrush. He uses the brush to temporarily clear the impact areas of blood and debris, thus tending to eliminate the possibility of recording two holes resting side by side as a single wound or mistaking a wound formed by a wood splinter as a wound formed by a bullet. Having determined this, he flips the handle of the brush between his index and middle finger, transfers the clipboard from his right to his left hand, carefully avoids the contact of paper to blood, rests the board on his left knee and writes. The fourth man shadows the third, his part to mark the locations of the holes schematically onto a large yellow sheet of paper already containing the drawn outlines of ten figures. When these two men eventually reach the prodigal tenth figure, their efficient routine slumps. The tiny brush flutters like a confused butterfly above the body, unsure of its landing place. Pens are immobile; paper remains unblemished. The two men shrug and a half-hearted attempt is made to brush away some of the now-coagulating blood. The action is quickly abandoned, though, and a notation is made by the third man which is, at best, a feeble approximation of the actual number of holes. The fourth man merely takes his pen and strokes a large X through the outline.

Gathering near the door, each of the four men verifies the completeness of the others. The man with the camera points to the tenth drawn outline, points to the figure on the floor, then laughs as the third and fourth men pocket their pens and dismiss personal responsibility with an explanation of hands — upraised, waving, their fingers firing blame in every direction except upon themselves. They check their watches, then more laughter as the group turns, slaps shoulders and exits.

The room is square and windowless. White prevails: white ceramic floor, white plastic walls, white ceiling. Only the presence of fluorescent lighting allows for a faint blue glow to emanate from the otherwise pale and antiseptic setting.

A single door blemishes one white wall and opposite this, off-centre, near the back corner of the room, a rectangular table is situated surrounded by ten figures, four on each side and one at either end. The conversation appears casual. There are no pens or papers to suggest a business meeting. Elbows rest on the pale arborite, hands support chins, stroke beards or simply stir the air. An odd head occasionally turns and glances about the room. There is no semblance of order, no items which might indicate leadership — neither itinerary, nor special seat, no gavel. Except for the table, ten chairs and ten figures the room is bare and, to disturb the silence, the murmur of a fan and ten voices — calm, dim, textureless — voices as might be heard in any waiting room, mingling with the air, clinging to the ceiling, unable to generate enough substance to form a shadow.

When the door splinters, so the calm glass of the room shatters.

Words, half-words, melt down the corners of mouths. Blood pumps, igniting cheeks and foreheads. Pores steam open, flesh dissolves; muscles, tendons tingle and jump spasmodically. Every head twists toward the door. All eyes report the entry of four men who place themselves strategically between the table and the open door. Revolvers raise, fix at eye level; gloved fingers squeeze. Figures at the table collapse as breath escapes through tiny holes drilled in throats and foreheads. Some attempt to rise but are snuffed halfway, their bodies blown backward, tipping out of their chairs. Others remain seated, slump awkwardly, a few sliding onto the floor. Two figures manage a step. One is hit and drops in a heap. The second falls to his knees, crawls a few feet, stretches his arms skyward in a sort of prayer and is snuffed out.

The four gunmen merge at the door, each checking his watch. A note is made on a small pad. A smile almost forms on the lips of one man but erases when a groan is heard from across the room. "Damn!" A revolver slips from its holster, aligns the sound and fires twice. There is a second of silence. "Damn it all!" The four again check their watches. A correction is made on the notepad. The men exit.

The room is square and windowless. White prevails: white ceramic floor, white plastic walls, white ceiling. Only the presence of fluorescent lighting allows for a faint blue glow to emanate from the otherwise pale and antiseptic setting.

A single door blemishes one wall and it hangs open, the wood split and shattered, as if forced by heavy boots. Four men enter pushing a large wheeled bin. One fellow halts immediately beside the massive figure lying spread-eagle nearest the door. He places his hands on his hips, mutters something indiscernible and joins the others beside the bin. "We'll save that one for last." They mumble agreement and begin emptying the bin of its contents: plastic sheets, nylon ropes, tape, mops, wash cloths, disinfectant and buckets of hot, sudsy water. From their white, uniformed pockets they produce gloves, rubberize their hands and start separating the stilled figures. Systematically they stretch the forms horizontally on the floor into a sort of prostrate attention, spines laid straight, arms pressed tight along the sides. Strands of looped nylon cord are utilized to strap the hands across stomachs and to tie the ankles together. Once strapped, each body is rolled onto a plastic sheet then bundled, bound in tape and piled three abreast, one layer atop another, inside the bin. After disposing of nine bundles in this fashion, the four men turn their attention to the one remaining figure. At first, there is some discussion that the last plastic sheet is too small to contain the giant but they discover that by having two men stretch the plastic while a third presses down on the body and the fourth quickly tapes, the body could effectively be wrapped and bound. Not so simple was the matter of lifting the body off the floor, onto their shoulders, above their heads and into the bin. Requiring a few false starts, some rearranging of positions, the body slipping heavily to the floor twice and almost three or four times, they manage to finally heave the bulky thing onto the pile. With much heavy breathing and mopping of brows, the four congratulate themselves and continue with the rest of the cleanup. Particles of wood, flesh and bone are swept up and deposited in a bucket. Blood is wiped, scrubbed, sponged and squeezed into a second plastic container. Once again spotless, the entire area is dis-infected and everything loaded back onto the bin or carried by hand outside the door. Next, the room is put back in order, the furniture removed and replaced with one rectangular table set off-centre, near the back corner and ten chairs, four on each side and one at either end of the table. The four men take one final glance at the room, check notepad, watches, nod approval, slap shoulders and exit.

   The room is square and windowless. White prevails: white ceramic floor, white plastic walls, white ceiling. Only the presence of fluorescent lighting allows for a faint blue glow to emanate from the otherwise pale and antiseptic setting.
   A single door blemishes one white wall and opposite this, off-centre, near the back corner of the room, a rectangular table is situated surrounded by ten figures, four on each side and one at either end. The conversation appears casual. There are no papers or pens to suggest a business meeting. Elbows rest on the pale arborite, hands support

chins, stroke beards or simply stir the air. An odd head occasionally turns and glances about the room. There is no semblance of order, no items which might indicate leadership, neither itinerary, nor special seat, nor gavel. Except for the table, ten chairs and ten figures the room is bare and, to disturb the silence, the murmur of a fan and ten — calm, dim, textureless — voices as might be heard in any waiting room, mingling with the air, clinging to the ceiling, unable to generate enough substance to form a shadow.

When the door splinters, so the calm glass of the room shatters. Words, half-words, melt down the corners of mouths. Blood pumps, igniting cheeks and foreheads. Pores steam open, flesh dissolves; muscles, tendons tingle and jump spasmodically. Every head twists toward the door. All eyes report the entry of four men who place themselves strategically between the table and the open door. Revolvers raise, fix at eye level; gloved fingers squeeze. Figures at the table collapse as breath escapes through tiny holes drilled in throats and foreheads. Some attempt to rise but are snuffed halfway. A few dive, try to disappear beneath the table but the gunfire is too rapid, the gunmen too precise — death nabs the fugitives fleeing, crouching and drags them to the floor. In quick succession the figures are bagged and it is only their stillness which causes the firing to stop, the revolvers to retire to their holsters. The four gunmen back toward the door, check watches, scribble a note onto a pad, face each other, face the room, then grin, slap shoulders and exit. There is no longer any movement in the room and the only sound is the murmur of a fan and the applause of feet padding down the hallway.

SCENE AT A BUS STOP

A young woman stands across the street, waiting, apparently, for a bus. She is on her way someplace. Out of town. This much is certain. The bus stop is not for local traffic. A purse hangs from her shoulder. There is a small travel bag at her feet. A short trip, one would suppose, or, having already made her visit, returning home. Is she pretty? It is difficult to tell. She is across the street. She is bundled in a long, heavy coat for the cool, damp morning. My eyes are not as sharp as they once were. She appears as if she might be pretty. Attractive, at least. Tallish. Slim. Dark hair. She wears a pair of stylish red boots, which leads one to suspect that... but, does it really matter? Pretty or not? Her manner is calm. When she looks at her watch (as she is now doing), it is not in a way that indicates a problem. It is more a reflex. It is obvious that she has every confidence that the bus will arrive just as the hands of the watch close in on the scheduled time. She opens her purse, pulls out a cigarette and a lighter. She lights the cigarette. She inhales. She exhales. There is at least this much time before the expected bus. Time for a cigarette. She takes a deep breath. She shivers. She smiles. Can her breasts be seen to rise beneath the coat? Really, such questions. No. The coat is too heavy or else her breasts too small. Nothing unusual. A young woman waiting for a bus. I am about to turn away, to resume my business, when a second young woman approaches the stop. Even at a quick glance, she appears to be the complete opposite of the other woman, both in dress and manner. She wears jeans, a light blouse and sneakers. Her hair is blonde, dishevelled. Her movements are tentative, jerky, fearful.

Her hands stretch out, retreat, cover her mouth, trace her face, tug at strands of her blowing hair. Her lips part as if to speak, but she says nothing. She must be cold. She wraps her arms around herself; rubs her elbows and shoulders with her fingers. She has a white envelope sticking out of her back pocket. As she nears the first woman, her actions become more withdrawn, though her eyes betray an intensity that evidences recognition. The first woman has not yet seen the second woman, or, if she has, she does not respond. Calmly, she smokes, taps the ash from the tip of her cigarette with a practised finger and stares ahead. The second woman is now situated directly behind the first. It's like a scene out of the movies. You wait for it. The first woman finally senses the presence of the second woman, except, unlike the movies, she does not turn around; there is no flash of recognition leading to some emotional purgation. Instead, the first woman merely flicks her cigarette to the pavement, crushes it methodically with the toe of one stylish red boot, looks at her watch and turns her gaze in the direction of the oncoming bus. She is in no mood for confrontation, this much is clear. The second woman also notices the bus; notices the first woman bend to pick up the small travel bag, and so she also reaches out toward the bag, but stops short. The first woman wraps her hand around the bag handle and resumes her erect pose. The second woman makes a move with her hand toward the first woman's shoulder, but again stops short. Her fingers contract; her face contorts. She appears about to cry. Does she? Perhaps a few tears escape. It's impossible to be sure. Certainly, her entire frame is agonized. She snatches the envelope from her pocket and attempts to jam it into the other woman's hand, the hand gripping the small travel bag, but the first woman only clenches the handle tighter so that the envelope almost slips to the ground. Almost, except that the second woman sinks to her knees, manages to secure the envelope in one hand and the hand of the first woman with the other. Both women freeze. The bus nears. The first woman unlocks her fingers, allowing enough space between the tips and the handle to receive the envelope. The bus pulls up. The bus stops. The bus departs. Only the second woman remains on the sidewalk. She looks so sad, so broken; her limbs are twisted in a way that is not quite human — she is a creature of rags and tears. In an hour, the first woman will open the envelope and read the letter. In an hour, the second woman will be dead.

But, no — the first woman still stands at the bus stop smoking her cigarette. There is no second woman. The bus arrives. The bus departs. Then there is simply the image.

Those red boots.

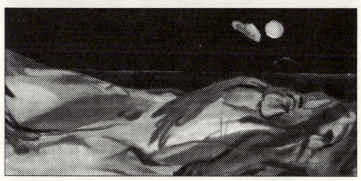

Three Sketches Toward a Self-Portrait by Sigmund Freud:
White • Red • Black

WHITE

We'd been invited over for dinner with Tom and Patty. Their kids had gathered with ours in the afternoon and would spend the evening with a sitter. It was nice. Almost like the old days. It was a Saturday and the two had spent the day preparing a spread of vegetarian dishes. Tom had turned vegetarian a few months back and Patty had followed suit.

Red meat clogs the arteries, said Tom. Be dead of a heart attack before you're fifty. Plus it's full of toxic chemicals. The same with chicken and fish. If they don't kill you outright, they give you some kind of cancer down the road.

The story wasn't new to me. Susan, my wife, had become a vegetarian around the same time. In fact, both Tom and Sue were heavily into the New Age thing and were even taking a few courses together: consciousness raising, developing innate psychic powers, discovering the eternal God/Spirit within — that sort of thing. Judging from certain remarks made at the house, I suspected that Patty was so-so about the whole business and was willing to go along with it so long as things didn't get "too far out." Me? I thought that most of it was a crock, though it did have its slightly amusing side. I figured if Tom and Sue were into opening themselves up to the universe in order to live forever in whatever way, shape or form, they could go for it. As for being totally vegetarian: no way. I found way too much primal pleasure in gnawing on a T-bone.

Booze was another recent no-no. Tom and Sue were into fruit juice now and herbal teas. It was up to Patty and me to do a job on the wine and that's what we were doing. Patty was actually getting quite tipsy.

"What do you think?" She sat on the couch, drinking her wine.

Sue was visiting the bathroom and Tom was in the kitchen stacking the dishwasher. I was casually checking out the art work on the walls and around the room. There were a number of God's eyes hanging, some bought, others appearing handmade, as well as watercolours and collages that also looked original. The collages had phrases glued to them, like: "The light is within," or "God is the way," or "I am a loved and loving person," or "Whatever you give you receive a hundredfold." On the fireplace mantle and on shelves and table tops sat polished stones, crystals, candles, totems, angel figurines, statues of Buddha, statues of an East Indian nature: human forms with multiple arms and elephant heads, and so on.

"Well," I said, "he seems to be covering the bases."

"Yeah." Pat had her fingers wrapped around the neck of a bottle and poured herself a glass. "Fill you up?"

I raised my glass to her. It was two-thirds full. "I'm drinking red."

"Mm." She tucked the bottle between her knees and clicked her tongue. I thought she might be looking for a bit of reassurance. I made a weak attempt.

"Our place is pretty similar. Susan, y'know?" She acted like she never heard me.

"Remember the walls?" she said.

I glanced around.

"They used to be a lovely cream colour, except that wall there." She indicated the wall separating the living room from the kitchen. "It was terracotta."

I nodded as if in agreement. Actually, my memory wasn't clear. It'd been awhile since we'd been over. The four of us had known each other for years and we used to get together a lot more often. Things changed when the New Age stuff kicked in. That was about fourteen months ago. I was unsure whether Sue got Tom involved or the other way around. Or if they had met coincidentally at one of the workshops.

"He's painted everything white. Not just white — semi-gloss. Even the ceilings. Look at it — you can see your reflection, practically. That set of beautiful black dishes we had? From Italy? He gave them to Goodwill and bought a new set. White. And those gorgeous red towels, made in France, I think, in my pretty dusty-rose bathroom? White. All white. The kitchen too. You saw that. And the bedrooms. Every one. The kids were in tears. Really, Paul, it's like living in a hospital. Or an asylum. I mean it."

I told Pat that Susan had painted her office in the house white and that she mentioned something about the hall. Pat stared past me, her eyes focussed on the expanse of milky walls and ceiling.

"That's just the tip of the iceberg," she sniffed. "Just the tip."

She was upset and the wine wasn't helping. I didn't know what to say; there was nothing I could say. I tried to be funny. "I suppose there are worse things Tom could be doing with his time." She never cracked a smile, but shot a look at me. I was afraid she was going to ask me what I meant by my remark, specifically, whereas it was only a statement thrown out for lack of anything else to say and meaning nothing in particular. I raised my glass to my lips.

"Has she tried to heal you yet?" Pat scrunched up her face, as if in pain.

"What was that?"

"Tom thinks he's a healer. He thinks he's in contact with spirit guides and medicine men and guardians and whatever. Dead people. He thinks he can tell what's wrong with someone by the colour of their aura."

"He's tried that on you?"

"Oh, yeah."

"What's wrong with you?"

"Oh, you know — I don't love myself, I don't have God in my heart, I'm still carrying baggage from my childhood and my past lives, so my aura's chock-full of ugly, black shit. Consequently, my mind and my soul and my internal organs and my life are a total screw-up. I'm outside God's grace." Pat finished the white and laid the empty bottle on the floor.

"She hasn't mentioned anything." Again, I tried to lighten the mood. "Maybe I'm OK."

"Nobody's OK, Paul. That's the deal. That's how it works." She raised her eyebrows at me. "Hm?"

It was all beginning to sound entirely too conspiratorial. An us-or-them situation. Pat was an intelligent woman. She taught computer courses at a local technical school, yet, here she was, reduced to lamenting the loss of her bath towels.

"God Paul — I loved those red towels. And my dusty-rose bathroom."

I wanted to dismiss Pat's fears — and it was fear that I was sensing — but clips from the horror flick *Invasion of the Body Snatchers* kept running through my head. Our respective spouses were going through major changes and no denying it. The dishwasher suddenly fired up and Tom joined us. Sue walked in beside him.

"How are you kids doing?" smiled Tom. "Getting along." Sue also smiled.

"Fine." I lied. "I was just taking in the art work." I stepped over to a musical instrument comprised of a wood frame containing varied lengths of hollow metal cylinders. There was a stick with a padded end laying across the cylinders. I picked it up with my free hand.

"Go ahead," grinned Tom. "Give it a try." Sue grinned, urging me on with a wave of her fingers. Pat got up and headed to the kitchen. "You can't make a mistake. Wherever you hit, you create music. We're taught to believe that musical talent only resides in a special few when, in reality, we are all capable of creating beautiful music."

I'd had this conversation before with Sue when she was "creating" her collages. My general attitude was, if we are all artists, then no one is an artist. Sure, I could cut and paste bits of paper and whatnot to a board and call it art the same as the next guy, but I wouldn't compare the piece to a Picasso or a Matisse. Sue said that I was a victim of my bourgeois, capitalist upbringing and that the only way to overcome my misplaced attitude and move on was to realize that, because my work emanated from me as an innately creative individual, then it (and I by association, I gathered) was every bit as brilliant and valuable as any so-called real artist. You may be right, I told her, but try and persuade the guy with the gavel.

"I'll pass," I said, and replaced the stick. From the kitchen came the sound of a cork squeezing from a bottle neck. Tom and Sue cocked their heads in the direction of the pop, then back to one another. They gave each other what might be called a knowing glance. The film in my head switched reels, from *Invasion of the Body*

Snatchers to *The Stepford Wives*. It was really quite chilling.

"That sounds like a good idea," I said. I joined Pat in the kitchen and we returned together, each carrying a fresh bottle. We sat on the couch and filled our glasses. Tom and Sue remained standing across from us. Something was up, no doubt. Pat shifted in the cushions. Her wine tipped and sloshed onto the arm of the couch. She turned to me and shrugged.

"Fuck it," she said. "They're both white."

I had never heard Pat use that word before. She caught me staring and shrugged again. I shrugged back and we both let out a little laugh, as though the spilled wine was to be our secret. Pat's eyes were puffy and her lips were having trouble forming words. I went to pick up my glass and there was Tom and Sue, still grinning like a pair of stuffed monkeys.

"Paul? Patty?" said Sue. "Tom and I have an announcement."

Tom gave Sue the go-ahead. "We have discovered, over the course of time and over much soul-searching and self-becoming, that we are kindred spirits and very much in love." Sue slipped her arm through Tom's and he pressed her wrist.

I don't know why, but the first thing that struck me was the word "discovered," like what Columbus did to America and how that turned out. Then "the course of time," "soul-searching and self-becoming" and finally "kindred spirits very much in love." It occurred to me that after employing such a couched sentence to admit their indiscretion, it was possible that they were expecting some sort of congratulations. I mean, the two were still beaming and showed no outward signs of either embarrassment or remorse. For my part, I was somewhat stunned and could only look at them with a sort of bemused silence. Pat, on the other hand, began to quiver through her entire body. Her jaw dropped, her lips trembled and a succession of tiny hiccups struggled their way up from her diaphragm to her throat. The dam was about to break.

"Pat?" smiled Susan.

"Pat? Honey? Patty? Listen to us. Let us explain. When you hear everything, you'll understand. Pat? Patty, don't cry. Please."

"You see," spoke Susan. "Through the classes we've been taking and through our own self-discovery process and contact with the spirit world, we've come to realize that we have known each other and been together as lovers or as husband and wife — whether Tom as the man and me as the woman or vice versa — repeatedly over the centuries. We were meant to be united once again, but only after learning what we had to from you and Paul, just as you were meant to learn from us. Now the time has arrived for us to move to the next higher realm of experience." She took a breath, then continued. "You're probably thinking, what about the kids and the houses and the other material goods that we've accumulated. Well, Tom and I have worked out a plan."

Through her tears, Pat managed to knock back another glass of wine. I sat on the couch, motionless, transfixed by the absolute calm of Sue's voice.

"The four of us work and earn approximately the same amount of money no matter who is coupled with who, OK? We each have similar houses with similar mortgages and similar monthly expenses. We have similar amounts in our chequing/savings accounts. We each have two kids, two cars, a dog, et cetera. So, we simply exchange partners. Each newly formed couple takes over one half and we make minor adjustments where necessary. We set up a schedule around the kids so that they switch houses and parents on a regular basis. There's no problem with schools since we live in the same area. The main thing is that, under this arrangement, we will have similar partners able to pursue similar interests and similar goals while maintaining the social order to which we are accustomed."

I emerged from my spell slightly. "Are you suggesting then, that Pat and I become a couple?"

"Naturally," said Tom. "Sue's right. You and Patty have much more in common these days than Patty and I. It all makes perfect sense."

I had no idea what Pat thought of me as a man or as a mate. I found her attractive, certainly. She had a warm and appealing personality (tonight being questionable), she had a nice figure and exercised to keep it, she wore just enough make-up to look interesting and her hair was always in place with a regular henna to keep out the grey. Still, I never had any interest in her except as Tom's wife and as a friend. So, while the whole notion did have a certain uneasy logic to it, and while I couldn't come up with any immediate retort to the plan, I couldn't help but feel that a major flaw had been overlooked. Pat filled in the blank.

"Are you telling me that you've been fucking each other?"

There was that word again, tripping easily from Pat's mouth. While not quite what I was after, it seemed to capture the spirit.

"Please, Pat," said Tom. "You're overreacting. You've had too much to drink."

"Our relationship..." began Sue.

"I wanna know — are you fucking each other or what?"

Sue glanced at Tom, then tried a different approach. "What we are talking about, between Tom and myself, is a fusing of souls, of spirits, of psyches as a way of ascending..."

Pat's voice was firm and direct; her words pointed. "ARE YOU FUCKING EACH OTHER?"

"If you're asking if we've known each other intimately, in the biblical sense, as a means of furthering our spiritual union, the answer is yes." Through everything, Sue remained calm, controlled and extremely pleasant. She worked as a manager in a market research company and she was very good at her job. She was definitely in her element here. Taking an idea, packaging and selling it was right up her alley. In a strange way, I was quite proud of her performance.

Pat glared at Tom. "You bastard," she hissed. Her head dropped into the corner of the couch. Tom inched close to her. He too was calm, controlled and extremely pleasant. Damned if I wasn't proud of him as well, though I was finding it all more and more difficult to take seriously.

"Pat, honey..." Tom crouched. "Don't cry now. Everything's going to work out fine." Pat's back was heaving and muffled sounds ran up and down her spine. "You know yourself that things haven't been working between us." The sounds grew louder and I wasn't sure if Pat was going to have a fit or what. "Paul's a heck of a nice guy. You've always liked him. Think about it."

Pat reared back, but not in tears. She was laughing. Tom stayed near, smiling, though with some concern. "Pat? Patty? Honey? Are you all right? Are you?"

"How many..." Pat choked. "How many New Agers does it take..." Through the tears, the laughter, the shortness of breath, Pat managed to somehow blurt out the words. "To change a light bulb?"

Tom shook his head, as did Sue. "I don't know, sweetheart. How many New Agers does it take to change a light bulb?"

"Five hundred," she roared. "One to change it and four hundred and ninety-nine to share the experience." She laughed until she couldn't laugh any longer. Then she passed out. Tom stood slowly. His arms dangled at his sides. He took the glass from Pat's hand and set it on the table. I placed mine beside it.

"Thanks for dinner, Tom. And the evening. Very enlightening." Tom and Susan stared quizzically at each other. I leapt to my feet feeling extremely energetic; even sober. I grabbed Susan's arm, grabbed our gear and ushered her out the door.

In the car on the drive home, Sue placed her hands in her lap and meditated. A slight smile formed on her lips. Her face, normally free of make-up and pale, was flushed around her cheekbones. Her long hair was pulled back and tied behind her neck. Once jet-black, it was now veined with snow — her witchy look, she called it. Sitting there like that, she resembled nothing less than a contented Buddha, whether totally out of touch with the world or totally in touch with it, I didn't know. I do know that as her form appeared and disappeared beneath the frosty glow of the passing street lamps, it was as if she was a neon sign flashing an advertisement for something, bliss, maybe. She seemed unbelievably beautiful to me at those moments. I kept glancing at her out of the corner of my eye. I couldn't help it. I couldn't help myself.

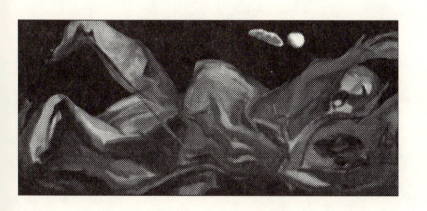

RED

The ad had appeared once a week in a local paper for almost a year seeking 18+ females to pose for an artist. Payment was forty dollars for a one-hour sitting. Some nudity was involved. Anyone interested was to contact Mr. J. Jacob. A phone number was given.

The studio itself was located on the second floor of a converted warehouse space near Queen and Lansdowne. There wasn't much of a view — an empty lot and a scrap-metal yard — but it made the studio private and the large windows afforded a fair amount of natural light. Walls were red brick and the floor was covered with salmon-coloured boards that had been varathaned to a bright sheen. Against one wall was a kitchen counter with sink and stovetop. Beneath the counter were cupboards and a small fridge. There were more cupboards above the counter. The cupboards, counter and fridge were all a sparkling white. Rather than freshly cleaned, they had that never-been-used look to them.

Furniture was minimal. There was a white, padded, straight-backed chair for the model. Beside the chair was a white table with a coral tablecloth. On the cloth was an open bottle of red wine and a bottle of port. On carving boards was a spread of food: cheese, crackers, bread, fruit, cold cuts, paté and more. Beneath the model's chair was a white oval rug. For the artist there was a chair, and, on a wooden table, arranged neat and orderly, were tubes of paint, brushes, sketch-pads, linseed oil, rags, a palette, jars containing sharpened pencils and various other implements.

There was no other furniture, nothing on the walls, no ornaments to make the studio in any way homey or lived-in. Clean, attractive and obviously not inexpensive, the place was functional, though perhaps a bit on the austere side. From a certain perspective, it could almost be seen as a cinematic rendition of how an artist's studio should appear.

A woman wrapped in a silken rose bathrobe poses in the chair. On the table beside her, the food remains untouched, the glasses unused. The artist checks his watch. He puts down his sketchpad and stands. He approaches the woman, places two fingers beneath her chin and tilts her head a fraction upward. He studies her face an instant, then slides the back of his hand against her right cheek. He applies enough pressure to guide her head a few degrees to the left. He removes his hand from her cheek, not immediately or all at once, but eases it across her skin, as if in a caress, though more practised and professional. He reaches to loosen the sash around the woman's waist, circles behind her, slips his fingers between the lapels and begins to remove the robe from her shoulders. Almost reflexively, the woman motions with her arms and hands, either attempting to stop the man or to assist him.

"No," he says. "Please." His words are firm, but not harsh. The woman's hands return to her lap. "I know the look I want." He undrapes her shoulders. The robe folds to her elbows so that her breasts are also revealed. He grips the nape of her neck with one hand while manoeuvring the other down her spine to adjust her posture.

"There," he says. "That's perfect. Don't move." He steps away from her, his head nodding approval. "You look very beautiful," he says. "Very beautiful."

The woman, in fact, is quite plain-looking. She has short, yellowish hair and nondescript, pale blue eyes. She wears an over-abundance of make-up in an effort to sculpt her otherwise sagging features. Her neck is thick. She has fleshy arms, hips and a pot belly. Her breasts, which are small, run down her chest like two uncooked eggs.

"Don't worry. You won't have to stay still for long. I'm almost done." He brushes paint onto the canvas. After a few minutes he tells the woman that she can get dressed. The session has lasted exactly one hour. He sets two twenty-dollar bills on the model's chair. She changes, takes the money and leaves.

"So, what did he do?"
"It's not what he did, it's the way he did it."
"Like what? Did he touch you?"
"Yeah, but not like touched me, y'know? Not like copping a feel or groping me or anything. At least…"
"Then what? Did he come on to you?"
"No. Not that either. It's hard to describe. It was creepy, that's all. It's like he's doing something to you in a way that seems like it might be OK, yet you know in your heart of hearts that something ain't quite right. Understand? Am I not making myself clear or do you think I'm totally off base?"
"I don't know. I'm not sure, I guess."
"It's like, after he undresses you — not undresses, exactly, just uncovers the top part, y'see, he says, 'You look very beautiful.' I talked with some of the other girls. He says the same thing to everyone. It's like he doesn't even know you're there in some ways, but… Or like there's no difference between one girl and the other. Like I say, creepy."
"I thought artists were supposed to be like that, cold and objective. You're just a sack of potatoes to them."
"This is different. There's a fine line, y'know? And this guy's walking it, let me tell you. Something weird's going on even if I can't put my finger on it. He must have money, though. Forty bucks for an hour and always two new twenties."
"Maybe he prints them himself."
"Bite your tongue."
"So, you going back?"
"That's the other thing. He doesn't see the same girl twice."
"That's odd, isn't it?"
"What have I been saying? Anyway, if you wanna go, go. Like I say, there's nothing I can put my finger on."
"I don't know…"
"You need the forty bucks, right?"

"Yeah, but..."

"And all you have to do is sit there for an hour like a lump and show your boobs for a few minutes. To tell the truth, I don't even think he sees them. Besides, after what you've just been through, this should be a piece of cake."

"Hmmm... maybe."

"Maybe nothing. Here's the number. Oh, he also offers you a tray full of food, if you're interested."

"Yeah? Did you eat any?"

"Are you kidding? It could've been drugged or poisoned or anything. Besides, I was being paid forty bucks to pose. I didn't want to be owing for anything more, if you get my drift. You decide for yourself."

"Yeah, thanks. I will."

"That's a clean bathrobe. You can change in there." He points to a door.

"Thanks." The woman gives the place a quick glance as she crosses the floor. When she returns, the artist is sitting with a sketchpad on his lap.

"There's food on the table, if you want. And wine. I have white in the fridge, or mineral water if you prefer."

"Great. I missed lunch." The woman's voice is hurried and a bit loud. Her hands pull at the thin bathrobe as if she's not sure that all the parts are covered. Whether out of hunger or simply as a means to keep her mind and hands occupied, she reaches for a cracker and spreads it with a thick slice of paté. "What's this?" She holds up a green leaf. "Some kind of lettuce?"

"It's arugula."

"Oh. Do you eat it or is it strictly decoration?" She grins and holds it next to her ear.

"You eat it."

She shrugs and pops the leaf into her mouth along with the cracker. "And wine, too?" She pours a glass. "You joining me?" Before he can answer she's filling a second glass and bringing it to him. "You drink by yourself, you're a drunk, you drink with someone else you're only an alcoholic. There's a difference." She returns to the table, covers a few more crackers with cheese and avocado slices. She slides a half-moon of melon into her mouth and washes it down with the wine. She quarters a pomegranate and rubs the fruit on her unmade lips. "When we were kids, we used this instead of lipstick." She eats another cracker.

"You're hungry."

"I told you, I missed lunch."

"I mean, you have a healthy appetite."

"Yeah. Too healthy." She laughs and pats her stomach. "I guess you want to get started." She plops into the chair. "Is this OK?" She points to the wine in her hand. "It's nice."

"That's fine. Enjoy yourself. It's good for a change."

"What's that?" She looks at him quizzically.

"I mean, you models — always on diets and such. It's good to see one who enjoys her food."

"Uh-huh, well..." She sips the wine. "So, I'm Ann."

"I know."

"Right. And you're Mr. J. Jacob."

"Right." He makes a number of short strokes on the pad.

"So, what's the 'J' stand for, Mr. J. Jacob, if you don't mind me asking?"

"I don't mind. It stands for Jake."

"Jake? Like in Jacob Jacob? A guy so nice, they had to name him twice?" She laughs and takes another drink.

"No, just Jake. My parents were somewhat capricious but they weren't downright cruel."

"Capricious? That's a good word. Is it, like, a polite way of saying they had a strange sense of humour?"

"You don't like the name?"

"It's a great name. Very strong. Very masculine. JAKE JACOB. Just doesn't sound like an artist's name, that's all. More like a businessman. Firm handshake and stuff."

"Steel magnate," he laughs.

"No, one of those sleazy used car salesmen." She laughs even louder. Jake's face suddenly grows serious. "I'm sorry," she says. "Did I say something wrong? I mean, I guess I'm here to pose, right? Not run off at the mouth. I can't help it. I get going and I can't stop myself. It's a bad habit. If you want me to shut up, just tell me. I'm sorry."

"Don't apologize. It wasn't you. I was thinking of something, that's all. It was nothing. Keep talking. I enjoy it. It's refreshing, really. I'll just sketch for awhile."

"OK." Ann grins then goes on to recount some of the highlights of her twenty-seven years, all the time sampling the food and drinking the wine. When Jake checks his watch, puts down his sketchpad and rises to move toward her, Ann realizes that she is nearing the end of her hour. Her body tightens and her hand crawls up her robe, clenching the collar at her chin.

"And then I recently broke up with my boyfriend. Or left him. I guess, really, I kind of... escaped."

Jake gently cups her jaw and raises her head. "Escaped? What do you mean? From what? Why?"

"Well, he kind of treated me rough. I mean, he wasn't the first guy that ever did. I seem to attract them. He was maybe worse. Slapped me around and stuff. Raped me, I suppose you could say, sometimes, if I wasn't in the mood or whatever."

"What did you do about it?"

"Like I said, I ran away. Left him a note saying I was heading west with a biker and he'd better not try to follow if he knows what's good for him."

"Will he believe that?" Jake continues to cup her jaw.

"No. I left notes before. He always finds me. But I can't think of anything else. It's more to try and hurt him, y'know?"

"I'm not sure."

"I guess I'm... just..." Jake runs his fingers over her skin and lays his palm flat against her cheek. Ann closes her eyes beneath his touch. A tiny sound inadvertently escapes her throat. "Mm..."

Jake turns her face a fraction to the left. His hand glides down her arm to the sash, which he loosens. Never losing physical contact with some part of her, he circles behind and slowly stretches his fingers toward the front of the bathrobe. Ann releases her grip and allows Jake to slip the garment from her shoulders. He wraps one hand around the nape of her neck and slides his other hand down her spine. She straightens and sighs; her nipples become erect; her neck and chest flush. Jake backs toward the canvas. His head is still and his eyes rest squarely on Ann's hushed form.

Now, she thinks. He'll say the words: You look very beautiful. But he says nothing, merely retreats to his easel and applies paint to the canvas. After a few minutes, he speaks.

"Thank you. You can put your things on."

Ann walks uneasily to the bathroom. When she returns, there are two crisp twenty dollar bills on the chair. "Will you need me again?" she asks.

"I make it a rule never to use the same model twice." Jake's eyes focus on the canvas.

"Oh." Ann stuffs the bills into her pocket and heads toward the door. "All right then. So long."

"But if you're interested... I mean, if you'd like to... I don't think I quite caught... Maybe if you came back once more. Could you do that? If it's not too inconvenient?"

"I could do that. Next week? Same time?"

"Yes. That would be fine."

"You've been going back there for weeks now. I don't know what surprises me more, the fact that he keeps asking or the fact that you keep going. I mean, don't you find him just too incredibly weird?"

"I think he's sweet. And gentle. It's fun to laugh and talk with him..."

"Talk? You mean he talks to you?"

"Well, not exactly. I mainly do the talking. He listens though. Like he's interested."

"So you don't know any more about him than the rest of us."

"I guess not. Then again, what's to know? I don't care about outside the studio. I like it inside. It's like being in another world. A safe world. Besides, I wait for those last few minutes, y'know? When he touches me so softly, and I feel that silky bathrobe slide down my shoulders. It's like everything up to then is foreplay and this is the orgasm."

"You orgasm?"

"In a way, yeah. I tingle all over. I breathe heavy. I look in the mirror after and my neck and chest are flushed."

"You're nuts. Or else you're as screwed up as he is."

"Maybe. The thing is, I'm starting to feel guilty about it. Like I'm taking advantage of him."

"Don't be stupid. He can afford it. You know he's still 'painting' other women at the same time, right? You're not the only one."

"I don't care about them. There is one thing though… You know how he always says, 'You look very beautiful', after he…"

"Yeah, yeah."

"Well, he hasn't said it to me."

"What — you mean he's never said it?"

"No, never. So I'm afraid that maybe… I mean, I know I'm not beautiful, really, but…"

"Forget that. You're gorgeous. You just don't know it. You're a helluva lot better looking than most of the girls he has up there and if he's too blind to see, that's his tough luck."

"The point is, these meetings have become my fix. I can't think about anything or anyone else. I can't help thinking that it either has to end or else it has to go further. But I'm also afraid of what might happen if it does go further. Maybe it'll ruin everything. And what does 'further' mean anyway? And why should it matter? And what if he gets bored?"

"You are in bad shape. You're not in love with this kook, are you? He's practically old enough to be your father."

"Not quite."

"Close enough."

"So, what am I gonna do? I've never been treated so nice by someone before."

"Can't go on, can't stop. Sounds like love to me. Face it honey, no matter how you dice it or slice it, you're doomed."

Jake unpins Ann's hair and allows it to tumble over her right shoulder. He massages her scalp, tugs at the auburn roots then rakes his fingers through the mass. He cups her cheeks and jaw from behind, twisting her head more to profile. Ann feels the loose strands resting on her breast, just above the nipple. She inhales, as if attempting to tickle her breast, her nipple, with the silky ends. Jake steps away, regarding her.

Perhaps now, she thinks. Perhaps this time he'll say it. Jake moves silently away. Ann hesitates, perhaps afraid to speak, perhaps not knowing what to say if she did speak. Suddenly, the words spill out, regardless.

"Why don't you ever tell me?" Out of the corner of her eye, Ann sees Jake cock his head. So, she thinks, he's heard me. It's out in the open. Like some kind of black, crawling insect. Nothing to be done except push on. If it's ruined, it's ruined.

"Why don't I ever tell you what?" Jake was stalling, either for his own sake or for Ann's, perhaps giving her time to withdraw the question or alter it.

"That I'm very beautiful." Even as she speaks the words, she hates herself for saying them. Who was she to ask this, to demand this, from him or from anyone? He makes her feel beautiful, isn't that enough? But it's too late and she plunges forward. "I know it's what you say to the other women. All of them. You remove the robe, you step back, and you say, 'You look very beautiful.'" She feels like a spy, or a jealous wife. How did she know? Who had she talked to and for what reason? Jake pokes his palette with the brush. Ann can see the wheels turn, though she has no idea what direction his thoughts are taking. He sighs, drops his brush, pulls at his chin. No words are forthcoming. That's it, thinks Ann, I've killed it.

"I have to tell you something," she says, "all these weeks... I've been taking advantage of you. First, I'm not really a model. Second, I keep coming here because of the attention you show me. I've never been treated like this before by a man; never been able to find someone, or maybe been too afraid to look or too afraid to ask. Like the whole thing seemed too impossible or I felt like I didn't deserve it." Unsure as to where to go from here or wondering if there was even any point in continuing, she stops. "I'm sorry."

"Please, don't apologize. You have nothing to apologize for. You see, I also have a confession." He rips a few sheets from the sketchpad and tosses them onto the floor. They contain nothing but scratchy lines and smudges. He lifts the canvas from the easel, flips it around and sets it in front of him. "I'm not really an artist." The canvas is dabbed and stroked with layers of thick paint. There is nothing discernible in the way of a figure, nor is there anything to suggest order or even attention to shape or colour. It more closely resembles an artist's rag than an artist's canvas.

Ann covers herself with the bathrobe. Jake can see the question on her face before she can speak it. "Look around. Do you see a painting or even a drawing anywhere. It's never struck you as odd or unusual?"

Ann studies the room as if for the first time. "Then, who are you?"

"You guessed the first day we met. More or less. Remember my name? You said it was better suited to a car salesman than an artist? I own a number of car dealerships. Other people sell for me, I'm strictly a mouthpiece. Which is why I can't tell you that you're beautiful."

"I don't understand." The story was unfolding, but not in any of the ways Ann had imagined. Maybe Jake was some kind of pervert. Maybe he was dangerous. She pinned her hair back in place.

"I told you. I'm a mouthpiece, a P.R. man. I've made my living dealing in idle conversation, false flattery and empty promises. I'm not talking about ripping people off or selling faulty merchandise, only that my relationships have, for the most part, been strictly on a surface level, and so, in the end, a lie. Because of this, I have difficulty speaking truths. I'm afraid I won't be believed. It's like the story of the boy who cried 'wolf.' Since I don't find those other women beautiful, it's easy to say the words. With you, I can't say them. Do you see? I can only do things for you and hope that you understand."

Ann rises, tightening the sash about her waist. Her elbow strikes the wineglass, sending it crashing to the floor. The contents spill and the two stare as a burgundy stain settles into the rug.

"Then what happened?"

"He told me that his wife left him over a year ago. He said he pampered her like crazy, gave her everything she wanted, waited on her hand and foot, but because he couldn't say those words that she needed to hear — y'know, like: 'I love you,' 'I want you,' 'I care about you,' 'You're beautiful' — she packed up and left. She couldn't understand."

"What's to understand? The guy's nutty as a fruitcake. So what about the phony artist bit?"

"He didn't know how to meet women; not on an intimate basis. He didn't know how to talk to them. He still wanted to be with a woman and care for her. On the other hand, he didn't want to be abandoned again."

"So, the women get the forty bucks, which they need, and he gets whatever he needs, an hour at a time."

"Something like that."

"OK, so far so good. But why were you asked back over and over?"

"Are you kidding? I ate his food, drank his wine, talked his ear off, took his money and positively glowed under his touch. Who do you know that's more needing than me?"

"Good point. Then what?"

"He told me I could get changed. When I got out of the bathroom he said maybe it was better if I didn't come back. There were two twenties on the chair."

"I hope you took the money."

"Yeah, I took it."

"Count your blessings. I still think the guy's a sicko. You're lucky nothing worse happened. To be honest, I've thought about calling the cops."

"What would you say?"

"That's the problem. You're not going back, right?"

"Why would I?"

"You have that look about you, that's why."

"That look?"

"Yeah. That look. That look."

When Jake enters, Ann is already at the easel, wearing his smock, squeezing colours onto the palette.

"There's a clean robe," she says. "You can change in there." She points with the brush. Jake hesitates, then grabs the robe and crosses the room. Ann pours two glasses of wine. She sips as Jake takes his place in the chair. "There's food on the table and wine. Help yourself." Jake sets a triangle of cheese on a cracker and raises it to his mouth. He empties the wineglass in a single draught. "You have an appetite. That's good."

She refills his glass, scrapes paté onto a cracker and hands both to Jake. He eats the cracker and drinks more wine. Ann circles behind him. She bends over his shoulder, loosens the sash and drops the robe to his waist. Her hands press his chest, leaning him back into the chair. Rather than remove them, she slides her hands up his chest to his neck, jaw and the lobes of his ears. She twists his head slightly up and to the left. One hand grips the nape of his neck while a second hand travels down his spine. Jake inhales, quivers slightly and half closes his eyes. Ann steps away, backing toward the palette as she eyes him up and down. She picks up the brush, loads the tip with a rich scarlet and approaches him. She dabs at his cheeks to give him a blush. She paints his lips, large and full. She colours his nipples and the circles around his nipples.

She reloads the brush with black. She darkens his eyelids, gives him long lashes and puts a beauty mark in the corner of his lips. She takes a step back and cocks her head side to side. With a second brush, she fashions a pair of white breasts surrounding the scarlet nipples. At every stroke, she watches as Jake's body heaves and trembles.

"You're beautiful," she whispers.

The glass slips from Jake's hand and drops to the floor. A second stain grows, then merges with the one already formed. Jake's eyes glisten as tears overflow the thick, black pigment and make their way down his cheeks and onto his breasts.

"You look very beautiful."

There is no stopping him.

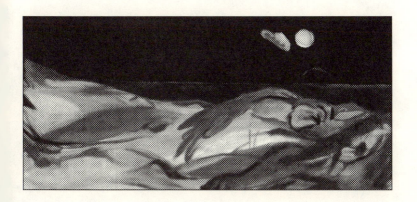

BLACK

Even a marriage is not made secure until the wife
has succeeded in making her husband her child
as well and in acting as a mother to him.
— Sigmund Freud

It's four in the morning, the end of September. Kelly had been listening to a Leonard Cohen tape earlier in the evening. She sings the words as she stares at the clock radio and listens to the telephone ring. It's a sign, she thinks. An omen. A miracle. OK, not so very big in the grand scale of things, she admits. Also, it's only two in the morning, early November. She'd been listening to lots of other music — Jimmy Buffett, for instance — and no one's fixed her a margarita. Still, if not a miracle, at least a strong coincidence and not to be taken lightly. Or maybe not. She wasn't thinking straight yet, and why should she? The phone rings again. Kelly shakes her head and lights a cigarette.

"It's either bad news or it's Stuart, which is also bad news." She considers the health of her family and the fact that the phone rings beyond any reasonable person's patience. "It's Stuart, all right, the nutball. He knows I'm here. He'll say he sensed it. Ha — where else would I be at this hour of the morning?"

The two had split about eighteen months ago. It was Kelly's decision. They had lived together two years. Two years was a magic number for Kelly in the relationship department. She felt that if you lasted two years without going crazy, then you'd make it to five, and if you managed to make it through five without killing each other, then you were undoubtedly doomed to spend the next twenty or thirty years wasting away under the yoke of so-called marital bliss (or martial abyss, as she liked to say). This was a natural progression and she was quite willing to fall in line with the pack, except she was going crazy and she knew it. Hell, she didn't understand how she'd put up with him for two years in the first place. They had nothing in common. She didn't even find him physically attractive. He was on the short side, flabby, had a weak chin, a large nose and wore his shaggy, rust-coloured hair tied back with an old rubber band. While she worked odd jobs to enable her to pursue her career as an artist, he never worked. He was thirty-six years old and to her knowledge he had never held a job of any sort, steady or otherwise. He lived off an allowance provided by his mother.

He was a perpetual student. He had a couple of MAs and two PhDs, done in comparative literature where he did his dissertation on some unknown 13th-century Italian poet who only wrote *verso sciolto*, an unrhymed hendecasyllabic line with the main accent on the tenth syllable — so, who cares? The other in math where his thesis involved applying Pythagorean theorems to the dimensions of the Egyptian pyramids and the placement of the stars in order to explain... whatever, she couldn't remember. The project was frowned upon by the department heads but was so brilliantly presented that Stuart was given a pass. Which, she guessed, was the story of his life and why she'd loved him in the first place and put up with him in the second — he was layered with so many magnificent facades that it took awhile to discover that, buried beneath, was simply a pocket of luminous but insubstantial gas. Try to grab hold and it slips through your fingers. Face it, she'd made the attempt and failed. Also, he was lousy in bed, which should've been the clearest sign.

The phone continues to ring. It was Stuart's habit to drop by unannounced every two or three months, usually late at night, after the bars closed. To say hello, he said. To keep in touch. He was almost always loaded and full of himself. Like it took him time to recharge his batteries and Kelly served as some sort of outlet for his raging energy: mentally, physically, perhaps even spiritually. "You're the only person I can really talk to," he'd say, "the only one who understands me." Well, yes and no.

The thing Stuart could do was make her laugh. She enjoyed his company for that. Not that he had a sense of humour — he didn't. He couldn't be funny if he tried. There was just something about him. Things he said or did amused her whereas they upset him. He could never figure out what was so goddamn funny. He knew he was never able to make anyone else laugh at anything. One time he told her that he'd attempted to list, first in his head then later on paper, the things that made her laugh so that he could try them on others — it was never funny; no one even cracked a smile. It was only her, so he gave up. Kelly would say: "The best humour is unaware of itself." Though he didn't quite believe it, he appreciated her using a bastardized quote from Goethe and, somewhat unhappily, accepted his role as unwitting entertainer.

Kelly lifts the receiver. "Hello?"

"Kelly?"

"This is she." She loves answering this way, in a formal tone, it always catches Stuart off-guard.

"It's me."

"Who?" There's a pause on the other end.

"Stuart."

"Stuart who?" Another pause.

"Are you kidding me?"

"Why would I kid you?" She goes through the same routine every time and he never catches on. He was brilliant, but not bright. It helped that he was also into his cups.

"You are kidding me, aren't you?"

"Yeah, I'm kidding you. How'd you know I was here?"

"What?"

"Did you sense it?" Kelly laughs into the silence.

"What do you mean? Where else would you be?"

"Precisely." She laughs louder. Stuart, she thinks, you are a riot. You kill me; you really do kill me.

"I'm at a pay phone around the corner. I've got a jug of ruby-red port. I thought we could order Chinese."

"How is good old Jack?" she asks. The phone goes dead. There isn't the sound of a breath. Good old Stu's scratching his head over that one, she thinks.

"Jack who?"

Kelly figured that if Stuart was drinking ruby-red port and was in the mood for Chinese then he was probably rereading Jack Kerouac. Stuart was a binge reader. Moreover, he'd get into character, either someone in the book or maybe the author. When he was reading Nietzsche's *Thus Spake Zarathustra* he ran around the city wearing a magenta cape with an embroidered eagle on the back, black with yellow beak and talons.

"Forget it," she says. "You can't order Chinese, everything's closed." She's made up her mind not to invite him up, not this time.

"Do you have anything there? I tell you, Kelly, I'm desperate for Chinese. You wouldn't believe it."

She believes it. He was always desperate for something, especially if the odds of getting it were next to impossible. When he was reading Bukowski it was boiled eggs. With Marguerite Duras it was salted peanuts. She could never figure that one; maybe the ocean. She wasn't sure. Anyway, she always kept a jar or two in the cupboard, for emergencies.

"I've got a can of wonton," she volunteers. "And a bag of dried noodles. And vegetables."

"Bok choy?"

"Lettuce." The idea of performing the impossible appealed to her.

"Now you're talking. Can I come over?"

"Sure. Come over." What the hell, she thinks, I'm up anyway and I'm finding him very amusing tonight. Two in the morning? Wonton and ruby-red port? Sounds very bohemian; very indulgent. Besides, I can get him to pose for my latest project.

She crushes her cigarette and crawls into her jeans and sweatshirt. She goes to the kitchen, finely chops broccoli, carrots, green onions and tosses them into a pot. She chops lettuce to add later. She pours in the wonton and the dried noodles, places the pot on the stove and turns on the heat. She takes two glasses and puts them on the coffee table. As the soup comes to a boil the door buzzer goes. She presses a button to let Stuart into the building. She spoons the soup into two bowls and sets these next to the glasses. Before Stuart has a chance to knock, she opens the door.

"How'd you know I was here?" he asks.

"Woman's intuition," she grins. She doesn't tell him that, for a small guy, he has heavy feet.

"Did I wake you?"

Kelly laughs and Stuart gives her a puzzled look. "No problem. I had to get up and answer the phone anyway." Let him mull that one over, she thinks. And it strikes her that it's not so much that Stuart is funny, but that she has a rather strange sense of humour herself. She laughs again at her own discovery, which really perplexes Stuart, as he hasn't uttered another word.

"Are those flowers for me?" Kelly's on a roll and knows she'll have to be careful not to be too clever, otherwise Stuart might just take his ball (so to speak) and leave.

He looks at his hands. "Flowers?" He says. "I only brought this." He hoists the jug.

"Good enough," she beams. "Enter. Soup's getting cold."

They finish the soup and make a dent in the port. Stuart has been going on about the current trend toward neo-right-wing politics, chaos theory and the question of negative space in the new wave French cinema, circa 1960s. Perhaps he's making a connection, perhaps not. He makes no mention of Kerouac, which is typical Stuart, him being *in it* at the moment.

"How's your mother?" asks Kelly. This works every time. She doesn't know why, for sure, but it always stops him in his tracks. Kelly met the woman, once, briefly, when she and Stuart were living together, over coffee, downstairs at a coffee shop. The woman said to her son, "I know she's an artist, but can't she afford a brassiere?" That was it. No hello-how-are-you-nice-to-meet-you, just that. Kelly wore a bra for her shit jobs, as she called them. When she was in her own apartment, painting, she was comfortable throwing on a soiled, tattered shirt and leaving it at that. She had gone down for coffee on the spur of the moment at Stuart's request. Kelly had ample breasts that were in reasonably good shape and she felt quite at ease with them. The last thing she wanted or expected was to be set upon by a tight-assed old woman over coffee. Well, fuck you, momma, she thought. She gave her lips a provocative lick and said, "Your son has never complained." That ended the conversation as well as any further meetings between the two.

"What has my mother got to do with anything?" He wipes his chin with his shirt sleeve.

"I'm just making conversation." She picks up her sketchbook and flips to a clean sheet. "Take off your clothes."

Stuart untucks his shirt and pulls the turtleneck over his head. Having posed for Kelly on numerous occasions before, the action is automatic. He's dressed in black from head to toe. It's not a fashion statement, simply easier. Especially when it comes to socks. Imagine, he'd say, trying to find a matching pair in the morning if they were all different colours.

"Mother's fine. Arthritis acting up. I had to give her a rub the other day. Doctors are quacks and those people who claim to give professional massages are in it strictly for the money. You're just another sixty bucks an hour to them."

"Pants too, Oedipus." Kelly chose her shots carefully. Stuart had difficulties making connections unless they fell within his present thought patterns or areas of study. If she was to pair Bernardo with sex-murderer right now he'd have no idea what she was talking about.

Stuart struggles with his belt; his pant legs turn inside out. He has an unwillingness to part with his glass.

"Stand up," she commands, and he obeys.

"Oh my God," he says. For the first time he notices. Pinned to the walls are charcoal drawings of naked men. "What's this?"

"My latest project." She sees that Stuart is more used to her previous abstract work, where body parts were pulled and stretched out of proportion so as to be scarcely recognisable. He likely thought her incapable of rendering an actual apple. In these, a penis was definitely a penis. "Are you jealous?"

"I don't know. Should I be?" He drinks.

Another man might have attempted to suck in his gut or flex a muscle. Not Stuart.

"You've lost weight," she lies. "You been exercising?" Stuart ignores the question, which disappoints her. He hates exercise of any kind with a passion, and she knows it. Has he twigged to her little game or did he miss the remark?

"Did you sleep with all of them?"

"All of them? No."

"Any of them?"

He is catching on, she thinks. Good. "I'm a free woman. I can do as I please."

"Not true. You're a romantic. And an absolutist. You're incapable of sleeping around. You crave unconditional love, for all of your laissez-faire pretensions and offhand comments."

Rats, she thinks. She hates the idea that he knows her so well, it limited her possibilities. "Maybe I've changed."

"Yeah, like the leopard changes his spots."

"Why should you care anyway? If I slept with any of them? You have your own life; you do as you please, don't you?"

"Don't play the martyr. You're the one who called it quits."

"You didn't seem to mind."

"That's not true. You hurt me deeply." He finishes his port. "Can I relax for a moment?"

"Go ahead." Kelly refills their glasses.

"So, what's with the rogue's gallery, seriously?" Stuart points with his glass.

"An experiment. I thought I'd get to meet more men, see if I could understand what makes them tick."

"And did you?"

"Yeah — they're all looking for their mothers." She smiles.

"Don't start that, OK?"

"OK."

Stuart's gaze moves from the pictures to Kelly. "You're looking gorgeous, y'know?" He has a slight erection.

"Are you sure it's me?" Kelly decides that, tonight, she will not be talked into bed. She's not in the mood.

"What do you mean?" Stuart moves closer, slides his hand under her sweatshirt and up her back.

"Maybe it's the drawings. Maybe you have latent homosexual tendencies."

Stuart raises the glass to his lips. He presses against Kelly's body, kisses her, transfers the sweet port from his mouth to hers.

"Mm," she sighs. "Where'd you come up with that?"

"You like it?"

"I like it, yeah."

"Part of my latest studies," he says. "North American sexual practices. I've been wanting to try some of them out." He cups Kelly's breast with his hand and gives her nipple a gentle squeeze. His erection nudges her thigh.

Maybe there's something to be said for book learning after all, Kelly thinks. She sheds her sweatshirt, her jeans and drags Stuart to the bed.

Kelly ponders the wine stain on the sheet. At least, she grins, we didn't break the bed. She puts on coffee while Stuart showers. She's naked except for a heart-shaped clip holding her hair in place. Stuart enters wrapped in a white towel.

"Thanks for last night," he says.

"Thank you. It was lovely." She kisses his mouth.

"I mean, everything. Letting me come over, the wonton, the talking... everything."

"I know. It was nice." There's a definite lilt in her voice.

"You want eggs for breakfast? Or, should I say, lunch?"

"I can't. I promised to meet my mother." He hurries to put on his clothes. Kelly stands there, observing him from the corner of her eye. She watches as his body turns from milky white to black. "I'm sorry."

"It's all right," she says.

"She's waiting for me."

"Never mind."

He approaches her. "She has a cheque for me."

"I said, never mind."

"It's the only way she'll pay me. In person. You understand." He attempts to kiss her but she turns her head.

"Just go," she says, and he does.

She takes the sketch of him and goes to pin it with the rest. She tries one spot but changes her mind. She tries another with the same result. Then another. She steps back; her legs fold beneath her; she squats on the red tile floor. She studies the walls, then the charcoal drawing, then back and forth.

"It's no use," she cries, and tears the paper into tiny pieces, dropping the white squares onto the red floor. "I can't make him fit. I can't make him fit anywhere."

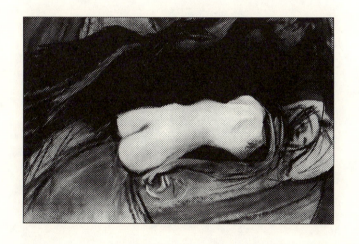

BEACHED

The beach. Any beach. Sand. Water. Rocks. A few empty shells scattered more or less haphazardly. More or less. Here and there. In short, all the attributes of a beach (feel free to fill in the missing parts; whatever is necessary to make you comfortable with the image: beach). And on the beach, a woman (as there is always a woman on the beach in cases such as this). She is young, naturally. And attractive. And well-proportioned. All of this, of course, according to the accepted standards of the Age (and, more importantly, the standards [desires? wishes? needs?] of you, the imagined imager; the reader, and so [again? still?], please, allow yourself to colour the picture to your liking [there is no one watching you; you are not being judged; this is strictly between you and the fence post and whether your hands are gripping the page or toying with a button or... whatever, it is up to you. Finally, it is up to you and the experience will only be as good as you make it]). The woman wears jeans and a loose-fitting shirt that's knotted at the waist. No. She wears a swimsuit; a two-piece; a slight bikini. No. The woman is naked. Naked, yes. Why not? It's all extremely tasteful. The glare of the sun off the green sea, the white sand, manages to blur the edges just enough; just enough. Yes, decidedly tasteful. Besides, the beach is deserted. The woman is alone. At least, she believes she is alone. There is a man (there will be a man), but not yet. Not quite yet. This is her time (uninhibited; at one with her surroundings; blurred at the edges; tasteful), not his. He will arrive (as he must arrive), but not now. No. For now, the woman is alone. The man, you might say, is lurking (though not lurking, that kind of lurking, as in "behind a tree" or "beneath a rock." No. Not lurking in that sense, but otherwise. Like an actor waiting in the wings to make an entrance [if that can be considered lurking, you decide]. Lurking but not lurking. Remaining outside the margin, so to speak. In readiness and non-threatening; definitely non-threatening. Not yet, at any rate. And maybe not even later; who can tell? One can only wait and see, even as the woman can only wait and see [though not wait, that kind of wait, you understand. The woman is not waiting for anything [[though maybe, perhaps, she is, or in some way is, we can't be sure]]). But even the hint of the man (a man; any man) is cause enough to make one wonder: what will occur (what can occur?), when the man arrives (for he will [he must] arrive)? How will the woman react? That depends. Perhaps the two are married. Perhaps they are friends. Perhaps they enjoy a casual acquaintance; a business relationship. Perhaps they have exchanged glances on the street; in a cafe; riding the bus. Perhaps the two are complete strangers. They might make love. Whether they are married or are complete strangers, they might make love. Stranger things have happened, I'm sure. Then again, one might just as easily kill the other. They may both be killed. Who knows? Anything is possible, after all. Well, perhaps not anything, but, a great deal. Certainly. A great deal is entirely possible. Them transforming into sea birds is unlikely, but not impossible. No. Not impossible. Given the circumstances. The situation (not, you understand, the beach. No. The beach is a given. It has been settled upon and there is no undoing this, unless [except], it becomes undone. Within the situation. The situation being [but, you understand [[you know, yes?]], the nature of the situation; its particular rules and the amount of play within these rules so that... but there it is [[in a nutshell]], and no need to explain further [[being fellows, etc., etc., so much time saved through a basic... well, shared experience, so to speak, an accumulation [[[that's nice!]]] of information forging [[[[even better!]]]] a plethora [[[[[no, now too literary; too cheap, but too late to go back, so forge...]]]]] of tacit agreements. This then, at least, is clear]). Them passing each other without notice, this, this, is impossible. What purpose would it serve, either for them or for the narrative, or for you? None. No, there is no avoiding an encounter — they must meet. He will be clad in a trench coat (what else?). He will be holding a medium-sized suitcase by the handle in his right hand (of course). Look! Here he is now! He wears a trenchcoat (though slightly more wrinkled than had been expected) and he clenches a suitcase (slightly smaller, yes, and in his left hand, it only figures, but, nonetheless, a trench coat and suitcase). We follow directly behind him. We watch his footprints form in the sand. He is barefoot. He is missing the small toe on his right foot. There is a peculiar indentation at the back of each heel. What could this be? It's all getting very exciting. He walks in the direction of the water; in the direction of the woman (notice, please, that the words 'water' and 'woman' each contain five letters — there is much in the way of significance at work here. The entire scene is taking on great symbolism. There is, perhaps, even the slightest hint of metaphor. I shouldn't doubt it. A beach, after all; a woman, a man — there is no escaping the implication — we have [we are facing], a history). Yes! There is great symbolism at work here, if one only had the time, or the inclination to pursue it. Instead, the foot prints, the man, the water, the woman, converging; carrying us along... how? Expectantly? O.K. Wonderingly, for sure, thinking: What will happen? Who are these people? Why is the man allowed to wear a trench coat while the woman has to run about naked? Why does the man even want to wear a trench coat on such a hot day? But is it? The day? Is it hot? The woman (whom we recently appeared to have some sympathy for, asking why the man should be allowed a trenchcoat [et cetera.] while she is naked [et cetera], and about whom we had [in fact], completely forgotten about, this being as plain as the nose [etc.], since it is only now that we notice) is shivering. Also, the sand is not sand, but snow. The footprints are now filled with two perfectly formed male feet. The feet are attached to a perfectly formed male wearing a trench coat and carrying a suitcase. The man drops the suitcase at the feet of the woman. The suitcase springs open. It is empty. The man removes the trench coat. Beneath the trench coat, the man is naked. He wraps the trench coat around the shoulders of the shivering woman (what else is there for the man to do?). The woman disappears inside the trench coat. The man folds the trench coat (and, presumably, the woman) neatly and places it gently into the suitcase. Next, he steps inside the suitcase and vanishes himself, closing the lid behind him. The suitcase is then swallowed by the snow (the sand?). The earth quakes. A tidal wave crashes on the shore turning the entire landscape a liquid green. The sun explodes. The water evaporates. The land flames red, then withers and chars. Heavy winds swirl the sky with ash. Then, the wind dies and there is nothing but blackness. The whole picture has gone to hell. Nothing lives. Nothing moves. Who knows how long it lasts? An object drops (from where? There is not even direction any more). An object enters? An object appears. It is barely discernible, yet there it is! It hovers, or else it's beached. Impossible to know. It is a suitcase (or it resembles a suitcase or it might as well be a suitcase). The lid opens a crack and a thick, white liquid oozes out and begins to fill the entire space. There is absolutely no preventing it until, at last, there is only this: whiteness, and nothing more. Not a footprint. Not a mark. Not a character. Only the faint suspicion of an undulation buried within this pale flesh; a pulse; a breathing; a possibility…

SELENE
— for Jerzy Kosinski

My life has been a series of arrivals and departures. I move constantly. Not in the sense of packing my belongings from one shell to another to begin a new home, a new life, a new job. The sense of motion. One foot in front of the other. Trains, boats, planes, cars. Uncertain as to where I am heading, I am equally uncertain as to where I've been. Also uncaring. I am not tagged or stamped, nor am I weighted down with photographic equipment, maps and journals. I bear no evidence. Quite simply, I am no tourist. I move. One might theorize that I move in search of my destiny. One might, but I wouldn't. The hard fact is that travel bores me, yet remaining bores me more. There is no life in the stones of the field; less life in the animated stones that work the fields: "For they had the possibility." Kierkegaard, I think. Bastardized, naturally. A throttled engine has more life. If I remain in one place longer than a day or two, it is completely by misadventure or thoughtlessness.

"I need a room for two nights."
"Just yerself?"
"Yes."
"Comes to $48 plus tax. Government's gotta get their share, eh?"
"I suppose."
"Cash or charge?"
"Charge."
"If I can help you any…?"

"No. I don't think so."
"Room's 207. Up the stairs and to yer right."
"Thanks. Do you have a bar?"

The rooms are the same. Always the same. Catering to the many, they please none. Off-white, scrubbable latex that never quite is. Resilient, multi-coloured carpet laid to endure. The furniture is dark and heavy. Cheap reproductions of landscapes or fruit decorate the walls. Anything that may escape the room is bolted down. No one is supposed to notice. It is necessary to cover more than we reveal. Parrotry and paraphrase. Powder and paste. Just as well though. Much easier to ignore. Much easier to forget.

"Another whisky?"
"Yes."
"You here on business or pleasure?"
"Neither. My car broke down."
"Serious?"
"No."
"Just passin' through, then?"
"Bit difficult to go around."
"What?"
"Forget it."
"Oh."
"Put a bottle of this on my bill. I'll take it with me."

It's a quiet room. No one fighting in the halls. No one fucking up or down or on either side. A quiet room. The only television is downstairs in the lobby. The owner is a duster fan. The windows are double-hung and painted shut; the door locks automatically. A very quiet room. Well-ordered. Symmetrical. Lying on my back, a view of the ceiling with its single harsh light flooding a bowl of dried insects. How do they get inside, I wonder? What keeps them there? I'll pour another drink and bury myself in the depressed white. Yes, a quiet room. Very quiet. I'll dream of six-guns blazing. Pow! Pow! Pow! The streets filled with bodies. Everyone dead. Except the hero who rides off into the sunset. Nameless. Faceless. Perhaps when I wake up it will be two days later and I can leave. If not, I'll need another bottle.

"Morning. Sleep well?"
"Fine."
"Room quiet?"
"Yes."
"We run a quiet place here."
"Yes."
"Car problems, eh?"
"Yes."
"Fuel pump."
"Yes."
"You're wonderin' how I knew?"
"Your brother owns the garage."
"I guess he told you."
"Mm. Where can I get breakfast?"
"Here if you want. Through that door. Or you can walk two blocks to Shirley's."
"Through that door?"
"That's right. Nothin' fancy. Just good food. That fuel pump should be in tomorrow. Won't take long to replace. You might decide to stay another day. We got a pretty town here."
"No."

Bacon and eggs. Bacon crisp, eggs over easy, yolks runny. Hash browns or pan fries. Brown toast. One slice with the eggs, one slice with jam, peanut butter or honey. Have I ever tasted an omelette? I drink two, sometimes three cups of coffee with a little cream and a little sugar. No juice. That's breakfast.

"Are you sure you don't want any juice?"
"Yes."
"Yes, you want some?"
"No."
"It comes with the meal. Orange, apple, grapefruit…"
"No juice."
"Pineapple?"
"No."
"I can't deduct it."
"That's fine."
"It comes with the meal."
"Yes."
"It's policy. No substitutions, no deductions."
"Mm."
"There'd be no end of trouble otherwise. Can't please everyone."
"I understand."
"Milk?"
"What?"
"I can give you milk instead. It's a beverage."
"No milk."
"Oh. Do you want the paper?"
"Is that a beverage?"
"What?"
"The paper."
"It's the local."
"No paper."
"And no juice."
"No juice."

Believe none of what you see and less of what you hear. Which leaves newspapers to line cages and wrap garbage. I knew a person once who drank juice regularly and that person went mad. More people die in hospital beds than die in hotel beds. There is no straight line between any two points, hence, no shorter distance. Paradox is the single proper logic. These are some of the yardsticks by which I measure.

"How was breakfast?"
"As expected."
"Good. I told you — nothin' fancy. Just good food. Did she talk yer ear off?"
"No."
"I thought she might. Loves to talk. Especially to strangers. I should've warned you. She can go on for hours. I watch TV. Doesn't bother her. Doesn't bother me. Everyone's happy."
"Yes."
"You're not given much to talkin', are you? That's fine too. Better, in fact. Entirely too much talkin' goin' on in the world anyhow. Where does it get you? It's been said by others before and better."
"Mm."
"That fuel pump won't take long at all once it's here. Then you can get back to doin' whatever it is you do."
"Mm."
"What line of work are you in, if you don't mind me askin'?"

Gunsmoke. James Arness is Matt Dillon ad infinitum. Chester warns that the Boyd brothers (Floyd and Lloyd) have escaped Yuma prison and are riding to Dodge City to revenge themselves against the man who sent them up the river. The man, is Matt. Matt takes the news in stride, loads his six guns and rifle and ambles on over to the Long Branch Saloon for a tête-a-tête with Miss Kitty who offers her sage and unaltering advice: "Matt, be careful." Et cetera. Matt orders (which he must and does), a beer which he will not drink. Chester grabs a rifle he will not fire. Doc sharpens a scalpel he will not use. Et cetera. Et cetera. Ad infinitum.

"Another beer?"
"And another whisky."
"I've met a lot of good drinkers in my day, mister, but you take the cake. That's a compliment. You've been in here the best part of the day and you still seem sober as a judge. I can tell with most when they're loaded. They go in opposites. The quiet get loud, the loud get

quiet. The slow move fast, the fast move slow. There's exceptions, sure, but that's the general pattern. Other times there's just little things, but I can spot 'em. Part of the job. Sooner or later they all start to stagger, they all start to slur their words. They get a funny look about them. Some fall down. I have to carry them out. One way or another they change. Not you, though. You're the same. You must have some powerful constitution."

I am not a handsome man, nor am I ugly. I'm not tall and I'm not short and I wouldn't call myself average, not knowing exactly what "average" presupposes. As a point of interest, if someone were to present me with an example of the "average male", I wouldn't know what I was meant to see. Having no permanent characteristics, I imagine him to be invisible. I am not well-built and I am not obese. I have no identifiable marks, no distinguishing features. I am balding, but this hardly separates me. Not average. Not invisible. As a trait perhaps unique to me it is said that I appear unaffected by alcohol. This may be true. I once knew a person who appeared unaffected by fire. The person died suddenly one night while watching TV. The cause? Spontaneous human combustion.

"Breakfast the way you like it. Bacon crisp. Eggs over easy. Brown toast and coffee. No juice. And — big surprise — I got it deducted for you. Know how? It wasn't easy. I went straight to the owners and said you shouldn't have to pay for somethin' you didn't have. She's a short, fat cow with a long nose like a rat. He's short, too, but skinny and has beady little eyes. You never seen a more homely couple. Suit each other. Both of 'em tight-fisted. Squeeze two bits from a nickel. You know the type?"

"You and your husband."

"Shoot, you knew! Someone told you. I bet I know. He told you, didn't he? Spoiled my fun. He told you. That's right. I'm May. Not short for anything. Just May, like the month, and you met Barney, that big mouth."

"He watches westerns."

"Barney and I figured what's the point of bein' owners if we can't change policy now and again. We set 'em, we can change 'em. It's not carved in stone. Especially for a stranger. I mean, you've got other problems to think about. That big, expensive car just sittin' in the garage, not able to move."

"Yes."

"It's not a travelling salesman's car, that's for sure. That's what Barney thought you were. A travelling salesman. I told him he was wrong. You don't gab enough to be a travelling salesman. You're a lot more important than just a salesman. Frank — that's Barney's brother at the garage — is sort of worried that this waitin' around might interfere with your work."

"No."

"Oh. Well, nothin' he can do about it, naturally. He can't carry every part for every car on the road. Right? Especially one like you got. Wouldn't make sense. Just sit on a shelf collecting dust."

"Yes."

"I got you a paper. I knew you'd want to keep caught up."

"With what?"

"Well, you know. The world. What's goin' on."

"Why don't you tell me?"

"What?"

"What's going on. In the world."

"Me? How would I know? I don't know what's goin' on out there. Wouldn't do me any good to know. It's not the local paper. See? It's the city paper. Whole big financial section. Stocks. Bonds. Real estate. Doesn't interest me but it must be important to someone like you."

"I never read the paper."

There are various ways to consume a day. Three square meals. Fifty-four cigarettes. A dozen or more glasses of beer, with as many whiskies. Salted nuts eaten one at a time. I breathe air in and out. I salivate, swallow and spit. I wash, comb my hair, brush my teeth, put clothes on and take them off. I cough and that makes a sound. I sneeze, blow my nose and scratch indiscriminately. I empty my bladder and bowels regularly. I nap. I perform actions either consciously or habitually. The order changes. Depending. The last action is sleep. To do is to be. To be is to do. As you consume the day, so the day consumes you. It is the same. It passes. Pow! Pow! Pow! The streets are lined with bodies.

"Morning. Sleep well?"
"Fine."
"Room quiet?"
"Yes."
"I told you. We run a quiet place."
"Yes."
"Guess you're in a hurry to leave?"
"Mm."
"Well, your car's ready. Frank called me not two minutes ago. You wanna leave this on your card?"

I was somnambulist to the morning. It wasn't early and it wasn't late. It wasn't hot and it wasn't cold. It wasn't dry and it wasn't wet. It wasn't common and it wasn't strange. It was every small town in the world and it was nowhere in the world. Anonymous. Average. A set of Chinese boxes. One bigger than one and smaller than another. The quickest draw in the west facing the next quickest draw in the west. And the next. And the next. Ad infinitum. Ad nauseum. The butcher, the baker, the candlestick maker. Interchangeable. Interlocking. Easily removed and more easily replaced. Generation after generation. Ashes to ashes. Dust to dust. The grand ordering of things. A joke that worms share. Dominus vobiscum. Domine. Domine. Shit. The sweet pain of the first cigarette smoke entering the lungs. I cough and that makes a sound. Another day.

"Why is everyone crowding around the square?"
"Gypsies."
"Gypsies?"
"Yeah. They just arrived. They're setting up."

"For what?"
"You don't know?"
"No."
"You never heard of Selene?"
"No."
"Never seen her?"
"No."
"Everyone knows Selene. Everyone here."
"I'm a stranger."
"Even strangers know about Selene. You must've been livin' on the moon not to know. Hear that music? It's startin'. If you want a spot, you'll have to move it."
"She's a musician?"
"Are you kiddin' me?"
"A dancer?"
"Sure, a dancer. Maybe even a witch. Won't matter if you miss it though. C'mon. Hurry."
"But, my car..."
"Suit yerself."

Brooms lean against walls. Laundry piles half hung and wet in the hampers. Meals are partially eaten. Cups of coffee sit to cool. Bicycles lie on one side, wheels spinning slowly to a stop. Bundles are abandoned. There is an awkward stillness to machinery in the streets, in the buildings, in the fields. Frozen silence everywhere except in the public square. Not a wind disturbs the scene or makes an opposing sound. All life is concentrated on the square; on the gypsies. Music thrashes the immobile wheat. Gypsy voices stir the crowd with a foreign language, raw and guttural. The people clap and cheer; sway to the ancient rhythms. A blanket is drawn open and a young woman — seventeen or eighteen — emerges from the folds and strikes a pose. She lacks the conventional attributes of beauty, yet she is somehow beautiful. Remarkably so. A Picasso nymph. Cubist. Long and slim. Features composed of sharp angles and flat planes rather than smooth curves. Her face is a chiselled mask, sunken, pale, with deep, wide eyes and pointed nose. Her arms are jagged arcs above her head; around her bony chest. She is mawkish filigree. A skeleton in flesh-coloured tights and wrapped in painted rags. Her mouth is an acute slash of red that is picked up randomly in her long, black hair. A fragile ornament. She moves and I wonder that she doesn't shatter into dust. She moves, though not until her body fills with music and it is not so much her as the music that begins to dance and she is carried along with it. Pain and joy in each movement; each movement threatening and exalting. Out of formlessness she creates form; spinning, reeling, almost falling — as the crowd falls along with her — only to stay balanced in some impossible position, then leap and continue. Her body slices through space, discovering its own patterns. She dives inverted, head bent toward death, then a shift, a twist and she is out of danger, disappearing from a spot and reappearing a few feet away, smiling, teasing. She brushes a strand of hair from her shoulder and even this simple gesture is filled with electricity. She bows; her chest heaving, her skin wet and radiant with a light very much of her own creation. The crowd is crazy. They applaud and shout for more. There are tears. Everyone is crying. I am crying. I lift a tear from my cheek with the back of my hand. I am crying. I am crying.

"She's collecting."
"What?"
"She's collecting. You have to put something in the basket."
"Something?"
"Yes. Don't you see? Everyone gives goods or offers services. For the performance."
"I don't have anything."
"Everyone has something. Everyone gives. See? Apples. Green beans. Bread. Cheese. Meat. Wine. Clothes. Wooden bowls. One person fixes the wagon wheel, another grooms the horses. Everyone gives. Here she comes."
"Lend me something."
"Too late."
"I have nothing to give. I'm a stranger."
"To have nothing to give is very strange. You can help load the wagon. That is something."

"I want you to dance some more."
"The dancing is over. Load the wagon."
"I can pay. I have credit cards."
"No more dancing. I'll be back. Load the wagon."
"When?"
"Two, maybe three weeks."
"I can't wait. I have to go."
"Go where?"
"I don't know."
"Good. For now, load the wagon."

It's been three weeks. I have difficulty performing the simplest chores. I force myself to shave for one reason: to be active. To fill time. How do they do it? What reason can there be for continuing with the same dull routines? The same dull conversations? What can they get out of cleaning, cooking, planting, selling, building, maintaining, tallying, managing? What can they get out of simply existing; keeping themselves operational? The westerns are reruns. Not just the same tired plots with the same tired characters. The same programs. The same faces. The same worn conquest of good over evil. The same boring ride into the same boring sunset. Meanwhile. Meanwhile.

"The gypsies are here."
"With Selene?"
"Of course."
"I have to bring something. To give. What?"
"What?"
"What should I bring?"
"Anything."
"But what? What are you bringing?"
"Ham sausage. We make it."
"I should have bought something. I should have been ready."
"I know! The wife's got some homemade pies."
"How many?"
"Oh, half a dozen or so."

"I'll take them all. Put them on my bill."
"Yes sir. Your credit's A-OK with me."

The music is much the same but her dancing alters, colouring each note as she pleases or as her mood dictates. She moves in a world of her own choosing; confidently, curiously, unafraid. She examines then uses or discards as if by instinct. No effect is contrived or forced. She is a combination of constant control and awkward grace, passion and reason, necessity and invention, innocence and experience. Always spontaneous. Always daring. She writhes and slashes, cuts and folds, trembles and flies. A jazz musician jamming with that most fragile instrument, the body. She whirls to the ground exhausted, soaked, gasping. Crowd response is unchanging — wild applause and tears.

"I've got something to give."
"Pies. What kind are they?"
"Kind? I don't know."
"Oh."
"Does it matter?"
"If it doesn't matter to you."
"Should it?"
"No. Put them in the wagon."
"Do you have to leave?"
"Yes."
"Now?"
"Yes."
"I want to go with you."
"It's not allowed."
"Why?"
"You're not a gypsy."
"I'll follow you."
"You will be killed. Hacked to pieces. Your body thrown to feed the dogs."
"Then I'll meet you. Where do you dance next?"
"Nowhere. I only dance here."

"No other towns?"
"This isn't the old days. There are fences everywhere. Laws. We live in the hills now. We come down when we need food."
"Then you dance in the hills, for your people."
"Why should I dance for them?"
"That's impossible."
"What?"
"You're compelled to dance. You must!"
"Compelled? I dance for food. I am compelled to eat."
"No. You must dance."
"No one must dance. Everyone must eat."
"The way you…"
"What?"
"…move everyone. You cast a spell."
"No."
"Hypnotize. You have a certain beauty that goes beyond flesh. Something magical."
"Everyone sees what they want to see."
"You dance with a passion most people only dream of."
"An illusion."
"You will be back?"
"Of course."
"When?"
"You don't listen."
"When?"
"When I am hungry."

I have a job picking apples. The farmer pays me three dollars an hour. "An honest day's work for an honest day's pay." Where does the honesty reside? The work is mean and monotonous and the pay is criminal. I sleep more and am more tired for it. With part of my pay I bought some stiff wire and a bag of leather strips. I gave the rest of my money to an old beggar. With the wire and leather I constructed a basket and filled it with apples. The basket looks atrocious while the apples are bruised from my constant polishing. When will she return? I'd pour myself a drink except that I'm off the sauce.

"What do you think?"
"Whatever you paid for it, it was too much."
"I made it myself."
"You've ruined your hands making that silly basket. That was foolish."
"No, that was from picking apples."
"Why did you do that?"
"I don't know."
"Neither do I."
"It won't do?"
"Anything will do."
"I'll try harder."
"Why?"
"To please you."
"Whatever for?"
"I don't know."
"You look for something that doesn't exist."
"Possibly."
"You think too much. They don't think and they're happy."
"They only think they're happy."
"And you?"
"I'm happy when I watch you."
"Are you?"
"What do you mean?"
"Nothing. I mean nothing."

I HAVE TAKEN AN INTEREST IN THE TOWN. I HAVE TAKEN AN INTEREST IN THE TOWN. I HAVE TAKEN AN INTEREST IN THE TOWN. I HAVE TAKEN AN INTEREST IN THE TOWN. I HAVE TAKEN AN INTEREST IN THE TOWN. I HAVE TAKEN AN INTEREST IN THE TOWN. I HAVE TAKEN AN INTEREST IN THE TOWN. I HAVE TAKEN AN INTEREST IN THE TOWN. I HAVE TAKEN AN INTEREST IN THE TOWN. I HAVE TAKEN AN INTEREST IN THE TOWN. I HAVE TAKEN AN INTEREST IN THE TOWN. I HAVE TAKEN AN INTEREST

IN THE TOWN. I HAVE TAKEN AN INTEREST IN THE TOWN. I HAVE TAKEN AN INTEREST IN THE TOWN. I HAVE TAKEN AN INTEREST IN THE TOWN. NOTHING. NOTHING. NOTHING. NOTHING. NOTHING. NOTHING. NOTHING. NOTHING. NOTHING. NOTHING. NOTHING. NOTHING...

"What'll it be for breakfast today?"
"I don't care. Something different."
"You've had something different for weeks. I've run out of something different."
"Impossible."
"There's only so many ways to cook an egg. You've had 'em soft-boiled, hard-boiled, poached, scrambled, basted, baked and fried. You've had 'em stuffed, pureed and whipped. You've had every kind of omelette. You've had French toast, eggs benedict and eggs Florentine. You've had 'em every way but raw and I don't serve raw eggs."
"Popeyed."
"What?"
"Popeyed eggs. Butter two slices of bread. Cut out a hole in the middle of each slice with a cookie cutter. Fry one side of the bread including the middles then flip. Crack an egg into each hole and fry. Lift the eggs onto a plate. Cover each egg with the cut-out hole. Voilá. Popeyed eggs. Any word on Selene?"
"Where did you learn that one?"
"I don't remember. What about Selene?"
"You haven't heard? But then, how could you? I just found out myself."
"Heard what?"
"It's quite exciting."
"What is?"
"We're all going to be in a movie. A documentary."
"Who?"
"All of us. The whole town."

"And Selene?"

"She's going to be the star. They want her to dance."

"Who are 'they'?"

"I don't know. A film company. It's quite exciting, isn't it?"

"How did they see her?"

"They heard about her. The whole crew marched right into the gypsy camp, pretty as you please."

"And Selene agreed?"

"Yes. I suppose. Why wouldn't she? Went with them to the city. We'll all be filmed here but she'll be filmed in the city. That's only natural."

"Why natural?"

"So they can use the studio. With proper lights and things. A real orchestra. She's going to work with the best directors and choreographers in the business. At least, that's what I was told. You know — being a film and all — they want to clean up some of the rough spots. Make sure she has the proper make-up and doesn't sweat at the wrong time. Teach her a few fancy dance steps. Although I never saw anything wrong with her dancing, myself. But then, what do I know? They're the professionals. We're fine the way we are. She's the star. That suits me though. I hate the city."

"You were told this?"

"You think I made it up?"

"I mean, someone was here?"

"Bright and early. Before you got up. Which isn't hard. See? I told you. Everything happens early around here. If you're a sleepyhead, you miss it."

"Yes. You miss it."

"The early bird gets the worm."

"Yes."

"By the way, how's your project coming?"

"My project? Oh, fine. Fine."

The shoot took six weeks, during which time I was interviewed once alongside my project. As promised, a preview screening was arranged for the town and a large screen and projector have been set up in the town square. There are even staggered rows of chairs to facilitate proper and more comfortable viewing. I stand at the back. The sun goes down. The film rolls and Selene dances. Perfectly. Oh so perfectly. She performs her routine without a flaw, finishing calm, dry, her breathing controlled, even. She is dazzling beneath the artificial lights: filtered pink and orange and bastard yellow; a touch of blue, a hint of lavender. We applaud — the only thunder in a perfect sky, as though the set extended beyond the frame of the projection screen, as though the entire event were staged; without rain, without tears. No moon. The moon bagged, abducted and raped. The moon strangled and buried by miles of cables and row upon row of electric lights. The moon gone mad with perfection, mad with death.

"You want to leave now?"
"Yes."
"Kind of late to be hittin' the road?"
"Yes."
"That was somethin' tonight, eh? Funny seein' yerself in a movie, hearin' yerself talk. 'Course they didn't show you, did they? Wonder why that was? Must've run out of time. Selene was beautiful, all done up like that. Our own little movie star. Best I've ever seen her. If I didn't know it was her, I wouldn't've recognized her."
"No."
"Well, sign yer life away! Here's yer receipt and yer bottle. Where you headed?"
"Nowhere special."
"Good luck. Maybe see you on the way back. We run a quiet place."
"Goodbye."
"Goodbye."

"Do you know what he did?"
"What?"
"He took a sledge to that chunk of marble he was carvin'. Broke it to smithereens."

"Probably decided he didn't like it. Don't blame him. Looked like a bunch of broken boxes glued together for no good reason. Do you know what it was supposed to be?"

"He told me it was the moon."

"Funniest lookin' moon I ever saw."

"I told him."

"What?"

"The moon is round and smooth like a silver dollar. I told him I didn't know what he was lookin' at, but it wasn't the moon. It sure wasn't the moon."

My life has been a series of arrivals and departures. I move constantly. Not in the sense of packing my belongings from one shell to another to begin a new home, a new life, a new job. The sense of motion. One foot in front of the other. Trains, boats, planes, cars. Uncertain as to where I am heading, I am equally uncertain as to where I've been. Also uncaring. I am not tagged or stamped nor am I weighted down with photographic equipment, maps and journals; I bear no evidence. Quite simply, I am no tourist.

NOTES

Is That You?
Depression: 1) a state of feeling sad; 2) a lowering of vitality or functional activity; 3) a psychoneurotic or psychotic disorder marked by sadness, inactivity, difficulty in thinking and concentration and feelings of dejection.

Passengers
"No, man must be naturally good or at least good-natured. If he occasionally shows himself brutal, violent or cruel, these are only passing disturbances of his emotional life, for the most part provoked, or perhaps only consequences of the inexpedient social regulations which he has hitherto imposed on himself.

"Unfortunately what history tells us and what we ourselves have experienced does not speak in this sense but rather justifies that belief in the 'goodness' of human nature is one of those evil illusions by which mankind expect their lives to be beautiful and made easier while in reality they only cause damage."
— Sigmund Freud

Dress Rehearsal
The text contains references to *The Plaster Geek* by Ernest Hardy (1912-1983), to the famous Pinardi episode in *The Cannibal's Story* (1947) by Duddy "Pot Roast" Bates (1923-1962) and to *Missing Persons*, a brilliant play I witnessed in the basement of a slaughterhouse in the late 1980s in Toronto. I've forgotten the name of the author.

Three Sketches...
Jolan de Jacobi, in her study of Jungian psychology, says in so many words: "The correspondence of the colours to the respective functions varies with different cultures and groups and even among individuals..."

"Spilled wine is a sign of happiness, but break the bed and all will have long faces."
— a Spanish proverb

What the Women Don't Know
"...must I, perchance, like careful writers, guard myself against the conclusions of my readers?"
— spoken by the character of Dr. O'Connor in the novel, *Nightwood*, by Djuna Barnes

Restless and Fleeting
This story derives from an old Chinese folk tale assumed to be written by the poet/philosopher Li-Len Kohn (584-650 AD). Here, a poor man walks to market carrying two baskets of ducks upon his back. The story was translated first into German (in which a poor man leads a burro carrying woven baskets to market), and later into French (where a poor woman rides a bicycle and transports eggs). Being unfamiliar with all of these languages, the story had come to me in bits and pieces via reviews and scattered party conversations. While there are (certainly) apparent differences in the exact details of the story, the message is the same: running behind schedule an accident occurs, the goods either run off (the ducks) or are destroyed (the baskets, the eggs), the poor person returns home empty-handed and various family members die of starvation or are sent to prison for being unable to pay their taxes, and so on. Meanwhile, the state continues to function the same as always, God is in His heaven, et cetera. I would suppose that variations of the tale are to be found in every society, in every century.

The line, "...as if to match a glove of space" derives from a poem titled "Rüd Apahls" by Horace Zass (1627-1672). The line is an alteration (really) from the original Brigandanese which reads, "Ahz ef toom ach ankluff es pache," which means (according to a review by Alman Pischoff in the *Globe and Mail*, April ?, 1990 [my knowledge of Brigandanese being even less than my Chinese, German or French]): The grass of the other side, green (or some such thing, it being so long since I actually read the review [or was I told by someone else who had read the review?] that I can barely remember. A cliché, at any rate). The whole point being, I guess, that there is this idea of endless, boring repetition which, for many (see Lucy Furness's illuminating book of quotations titled, *Burn, Baby, Burn* (1976)), is the concise definition of Hell.

The Regular

I was reading a news clipping from the *Enquirer*. It was taped to the cash register of Leung's Market & Confection, where I normally shopped. The clipping told how a Chinese grocer had suddenly gone "crazy" and began firing shots at the customers in his store, killing eight and wounding several more. There was a picture of him with his wife and two children. He was still cradling the rifle, was still surrounded by the slumped, bloodied bodies of the dead and wounded. He looked very sad. A caption had been written in ink above the article, it said: NO MORE GRAPE.

Notes

A tip of the hat to Richard Brautigan and Raymond Carver, both done in by the sword, too soon.

PRINTED AND BOUND
IN BOUCHERVILLE, QUÉBEC, CANADA
BY MARC VEILLEUX IMPRIMEUR INC.
IN FEBRUARY, 1998